Miss Lamp

Chris Ewart

Coach House Books | Toronto

Canada Council   Conseil des Arts
for the Arts   du Canada

ONTARIO ARTS COUNCIL
CONSEIL DES ARTS DE L'ONTARIO

Canadä

Published with the assistance of the Canada Council for the Arts and the
Ontario Arts Council. Coach House Books also appreciates the financial
support of the Government of Ontario through the Ontario Book
Publishing Tax Credit Program and the Government of Canada through
the Book Publishing Industry Development Program.

LIBRARY AND ARCHIVES CANADA CATALOGUING IN PUBLICATION

Ewart, Chris, 1970-
    Miss Lamp / Chris Ewart. -- 1st ed.

ISBN-13: 978-1-55245-166-3
ISBN-10: 1-55245-166-6

    I. Title.

PS8609.W37M58 2006   C813'.6   C2006-901978-9

for Mama

'It's okay to talk to yourself,
just don't answer your own questions.'
Stan Ewart, 1910–1992

§

Miss Lamp.

Miss Lamp shines.

A half-smile from Miss Lamp lights her hotel room like a yellow party dress. She left her sky-blue knee-high skirt at home, home where she strums songs on Saturdays, songs about chameleons, raccoons or not eating dill pickles. The stoop hits thirty degrees on a good June morning. She sings with shiny lips on a good June morning. Peach lip balm.

That skirt gets hot enough to melt. But it just shines bluer.

She lies in her hotel bed in the evening, sun still up, wiggling her toes free of the sheets. Dribbling a sip of juice on her flannel Mountie pyjamas, she caresses her neck and says, 'I miss my water pillow.' After reading the 'Major Major Major Major' chapter from *Catch-22* aloud, she thinks about insurance.

Her travel bag sits snugly beside the door of Room 32. Miss Lamp travels light. She flies a lot when that dental-insurance company retains her counsel, so she's well-read in dentistry. Her attaché case contains the latest news on the practice of malpractice, plastic-composite teeth, the benefits of freezing gum tissue before drilling and transcripts about her gentle, ailing mother, Abby.

Miss Lamp's belly grumbles in Room 32, barely halfway across town from her gentle, ailing crybaby of a mother.

'One more mission,' sighs Miss Lamp. 'At least the peaches are in season.'

§

The Cheque's in the Mail.
Ever since the dentist, Abby's finger is a real whack of volts.

Chewing gum makes her jaw ache. Her red lips quiver at the thought of the drill – she's pursed to sing like a raven with a mouth full of Q-tips. Cotton batting packs a statute of limitations, nerve damage and overmedication. The needle for her tooth fixed her left index finger just fine. Now it twitches during meetings where people look at watches, ask for phone numbers, go for drinks and grin with teeth picked clean of grief.

Abby's daughter picks at whatever's not nailed down. A real nattering magpie.

Abby's mailbox rattles in the wind. Sits on a post as straight as a sunflower stalk and turns up empty each day.

No payment for the pills she pops to keep her nerves in check. No new music box from her lawyer of a daughter either. 'I shouldn't have wound the crank so tight,' says Abby. 'She sings a different tune now.'

§

Service with a Smile.

For the seventh time since 6:42 a.m., Miss Lamp reminds herself that she loves the law and that grilled cheese goes quite well with warm tomato soup. She grins and picks at the fat manila envelope marked DELANO.

A crisp knock at the door brings a push of manila out of sight. 'Yes?'

'Room service, ma'am. Um, I'm really sorry, but we don't have any Campbell's Tomato Soup. But there's a Safeway down the street and I'd be happy to get some for you – it'll be five minutes or so. I'm really sorry because I know you asked for Campbell's Tomato Soup specifically and, well, we're all out, ma'am.'

Miss Lamp nibbles at a hangnail. His voice sounds young. Fresh. 'Oh. I'm not sure then.'

Room Service Boy knocks again, less crisply.

'Room service, ma'am ... Um ... do you still want the grilled cheese? Golden brown, wasn't it? I can go to Safeway, ma'am, I don't mind. It's my job.' Room Service Boy prides himself on customer satisfaction.

Miss Lamp clenches the nail between her teeth and pulls. Halfway to a crescent moon. 'Ow! Jesus!' The flesh underneath turns purple and red in a hurry.

'Ma'am? Are you okay?' He shuffles his feet closer to the door. The hallway smells of mothballs and tea. 'Ma'am, do you still want the grilled cheese? Golden brown, cut to corners.' Room Service Boy counts to himself. 'In four, with a pickle on the side?'

Miss Lamp removes a throbbing finger from her mouth. It tastes like a pretty penny. 'No. Not now. Maybe later when you have the right soup.'

Miss Lamp requires the right kind of soup.

The envelope returns to its place while Room Service Boy responds with a humble 'Thank you, ma'am.' Her voice gives him goosebumps. As he scuffs back down the hall, he sniffs at the armpits of his purple uniform.

§

Squeak Goes the Wagon.

Delano always hit Paper Boy with a pewter-tipped walking stick. It never occurred to Paper Boy to run away. He didn't run, scream or argue when he saw the heavy walking stick. Sparks flew when that walking stick hit the sidewalk.

'Stand still! I'm talking to you, boy! Stop leafing about!' Delano said, poking him with the cold tip of the walking stick. 'Do you understand the importance of *time*, boy? Do you know what it means to be *on time*? Oh, I'm not finished here yet.'

Delano coughed and spat feebly to the ground. A string of milky spittle joined his chin to the lapel of his loose-fitting mauve satin housecoat. Another jab bruised the pulp behind Paper Boy's sternum. The spit swung like a chain. 'We people rely on you for the facts of the day, boy. What would happen if everyone's facts of the day were late? Huh? I'll bet you never minded the global implications there, did you, boy? So don't start it now and don't start it here.'

He pushed hard on 'now' and 'here.'

'There would be chaos. Lots and lots of chaos, boy. Do you know what chaos is?'

Paper Boy uncrinkled his shirt.

'That's why I got a peephole in my door. And I use it too, so people like you don't start making chaos for people like me.'

Delano coughed again, swinging a hand into the calm, damp air as if to balance himself. 'Now give me my damn paper, you imbecile, and don't waste any more of my time. It's getting late and I have teeth to pull. Facts is facts, boy.'

Paper Boy thought the smelly, spitty man should use his walking stick properly – to help himself stand up. A walking stick did not belong in the middle of Paper Boy's paper-thin chest.

'You be on time tomorrow. Got it?'

Paper Boy's twelve-year-old legs lost their balance, crunching into the gravel driveway.

'Get up and give me my paper.'

He handed it over with ink-stained fingers.

'Stop shaking, boy. Why the hell are you twitching, anyway? Suck it up. I'm not going to tear you limb from limb.'

Paper Boy squeezed the rusty black handle of his red paper wagon, squeaking it away from the smelly, spitty man.

'Now get off my property, and don't forget to be on time, Paper Boy.'

Chirps from the trees turned the purple sky to red. Paper Boy checked his watch. The paper wasn't late at all.

§

Sprung Flowers.

        Sitting on the end of one of the two twin.
Miss Lamp rubs her right hand over polyester gardens. Not ᴊest
Western. The card on the side table reads WELCOME TO PEACH-
LAND HOTEL. Gideon's Bible rests in the drawer until she places it
in her travel bag. She hums a bar of 'Rocky Raccoon.' Plastic
flowers don't brighten up a room much either, but they won't
collect dust in her travel bag.

    Miss Lamp's cheeks itch when she craves Campbell's Tomato
Soup. Her afternoon nap will not come easy on a stomach empty
of Campbell's. Soup is good food.

    Room Service Boy's knowledge of grilled-cheese presentation
impresses Miss Lamp. Cut to corners, golden brown and not burnt.
Grilled cheese is art, but not without the right kind of soup.

    She nods slightly, picking at a clear thread from the pattern of
hyacinths pink and blue, orange-centred beige daisies and prickly
holly bushes. Her right fingertip finds this thread easy to wind.
Within seconds, the bedspread lifts a little. An artificial garden
freed from its fencing, she thinks.

    Her threaded fingertip turns like a tulip. She leans into the bed
as if to sniff it, snapping the excess plastic twine with her inci-
sors. Her adeptness at removing clothing tags proves scissors
obsolete – strong teeth will do. Her eyes reel in sleep.

§

That's What Friends Are For.

Young Miss Lamp sat drunk when her seventeen looked fourteen. Paper Boy, whose seventeen looked seventeen, passed out while she squinted. She watched him wedged in the wooden Peachland Hotel chair, in various states of undress, until the sun went down.

'Can we borrow your lipstick?' Serge smirked widely.

'And do you have any rope, you know, to tie with?' said Rick.

'Rope?' Young Miss Lamp searched through her purse, finding some Peach Pastel and a fresh box of minty Butler dental floss. 'Will this do?'

'Thanks,' Serge said as she handed over the floss.

'We put four Demerols in his drink,' said Rick.

'He's out like a light,' slurred Serge.

Blobs of pulp glued the lazy corners of Paper Boy's mouth shut. Serge pulled yards and yards of minty fresh floss from the little white box. Rick snapped it taut on the rounded silver cutter.

Young Miss Lamp had never before seen Paper Boy in a pair of blue underwear, all tied up with dental floss.

Hands and feet.

He didn't even wake up.

'Poor fella,' she whispered to herself.

When the two other boys required a dainty finger to secure the floss in a double knot, she said, 'I'll do it.' With a bit of encouragement, she wrote LOSER across his forehead.

Then she handed over the lipstick.

Rick and Serge took liberty upon his fresh white skin. Young Miss Lamp saw the coarse, dark beginnings of belly hair. FOR A GOOD TIME, it said, ROLL ME OVER. A brittle chest and peach air freshener.

'Poor fella,' she whispered to herself again. 'He doesn't even know what's happening, and only in underwear.' Young Miss Lamp freshened her seventh Captain Morgan and Coke, rubbed her eyes and returned to the foot of the bed.

§

Soup Is Good Food.

Leaving the sanctity of mothballs and tea to wear out his heels on the warm asphalt of the Safeway parking lot, Room Service Boy walks slowly, wondering why he buys Campbell's Tomato Soup for rich, stuck-up lawyer-types who talk at him through closed doors.

'It's my job,' he reminds himself to random passersby as they scuttle through automatic doors, armed with bags and trolleys. 'It's my job,' he repeats for assurance. 'Soup. Aisle 7. Next to soups of other brands, flavours and qualities. Pricing is not dependant on size. Adjacent to stews, vegetable and mechanically separated meat products. Microwave in foam for real beef taste. Scotch Broth with Barley, Chicken Vegetable, Cream of Mushroom, Celery, Chicken Noodle and Tomato. A healthy source of vitamin C. Make with one part milk for a creamier taste and do not allow to boil. Must be stirred continuously. Continuously.'

A film of fluorescent lighting bleaches the floor and Room Service Boy bites his lip before he gets too loud. White-knuckling the can all the way to Express Checkout 3, he spies a name tag that reads LUCY. She smiles at Room Service Boy. Her hair is yellow like the banana tray in front of her checkout and she has all the shape of a swizzle stick. He places the can of Campbell's Tomato Soup heavily on the rubber conveyor belt.

Banana Tray Hair's lips move along with the soup tin, closer and closer together.

'How are we today?'

Grumpy, he thinks, Burnt milk is unacceptable.

'Just the soup then?'

'Yes.'

'Working tonight, are we?'

'Yes.' Room Service Boy wears his purple suit to prove it.

'Club Card and Air Miles, please.'

'I don't – '

'No? Will this be all then?' Banana Tray Hair expedites her customers speedily.

Room Service Boy nods in agreement.

'Your total comes to $1.52 with tax. Do you need help out with that?'

Banana Tray Hair smiles at Room Service Boy again. The receipt for the soup belongs in his pocket. Not since his last time chatting with Banana Tray Hair has Room Service Boy heard so many questions in a row. All directed at him.

'We are closing in ten minutes, shoppers. Please finalize your purchasing choices. Thank you for choosing Safeway, and have a good night, Soup Boy.'

His cheeks match his purple dickie bow tie. He imagines saying, 'Now you have a good night too, Banana Tray Hair, ma'am,' but his tongue congeals the words. The best he can do is a squeak of thanks as he shuffles toward the yawn of the automatic door.

Back across the parking lot, he wonders how many ways a person could be helped out with a can of soup. After the 437 steps to the hotel, Room Service Boy spins through its revolving Plexiglas door, bounds into the lobby and shouts, 'Six!'

'Get that soup to the kitchen at once – he's closing soon.' The Front Desk Man taps the receipts for the day into a tidy ruffle of a square. 'It's for the shut-in in Room 32. And don't spill it either.' Room Service Boy never spills.

Sliding on the wet kitchen floor with a tin of Campbell's Tomato Soup in his hand, Room Service Boy eyes The Cook. The Cook grumbles about closing time while Room Service Boy squishes his soles back to the mat. With milk, he remembers, this soup is an excellent source of calcium. His lips move slightly when remembering, but not enough to cause a stir. He brims over all of the six possibilities put together, the six possible ways a Safeway shopper might be helped out of Safeway with a single can of tomato soup.

1. Banana Tray Hair pays for the soup.
2. Banana Tray Hair carries the soup to the hotel.
3. Banana Tray Hair opens the can of soup.
4. Banana Tray Hair cooks the soup.
5. Banana Tray Hair pours the soup in a bowl.
6. Banana Tray Hair delivers the soup to Room 32 without spilling it.

Of Room Service Boy's six possibilities for being helped out with the soup, he deems Number 6 least plausible, since she would probably spill some of the soup, marring his impeccable record of food delivery. 'The grilled cheese must be golden brown and cut to corners,' he says to himself. 'It's my job,' he repeats for assurance. The Cook doesn't notice Room Service Boy's lips moving at all.

§

The Tooth, the Whole Tooth.

Paper Boy woke before the sun warmed the room. He smelled of minty, waxy peaches as he writhed on the carpet in his blue underwear, all flossed up with nowhere to go.

Rick and Serge were sawing themselves to sleep.

He picked and frayed and broke the floss, along with one of his good straight teeth. A bottle opener freed his ankles, then his shaky fingers collected a thin line of red-and-white string. He found his pants and jacket beside the toilet. His soppy T-shirt was fit for the tub. He didn't look in the mirror, and he didn't look in the mirror of the Checker Cab he called from the lobby. He tried to erase the lines on his wrists. Silly doodles in red pen. Tracing gums with his tongue, he realized he'd swallowed part of a good straight tooth.

Paper Boy let out a crinkle, paying the cabbie slightly less than was due. Dollar bills, quarters and nickels. He felt thin and shy. Parched.

'That's enough, buddy. Don't give me all your damn change.' With a paternal glint, the cabbie continued, 'Go wash your face, and maybe you should sleep some. It's supposed to rain today anyway. Christ, boy, you don't look so hot. Should I take you to the hospital?'

Paper Boy hid his wrists with the cuffs of his jacket. He left the cab door open behind him, and his voice box seized up. A broken crank. Without a thank you, he spat blood to the curb.

He was missing his watch, a good Timex, with a band that buckled. His rubbery muscles sprang and sprung toward the river. The Demerol in his veins numbed his legs from the knees down. After the cabbie stretched his strong arm behind the front seat to shut the open door, Paper Boy turned around to wave, to check if his wrist still worked. An elastic band waiting to snap a question. A pensive palm bent slightly.

'You can't wear a watch now anyway,' he said to his wrist.

§

Hangnail for a Wink.

Between the creases of her pillow, Miss Lamp picks the sleep from her eyes. An itch on her cheek brings her left hand out from under her side. Congealed blood, skin and toilet paper drag along the polyester bedspread. She sucks in her cheeks like a lemon. Pins and needles tickle her immaculately shaved underarm, sewing themselves into the lapel of her collarbone. Her eyes blink wet.

'That was smart,' she says. 'I need a band-aid.'

Leaning over the side of the bed, she reaches into her carry-on, beams at her manicure kit and zips slowly around its corners. It's full of shiny picks, files, clippers, tweezers and scissors. 'Security is blind,' she says, pondering the possibility of hijacking an airplane with a pair of well-sharpened nail scissors. Just a glimpse of an emery board and her finger throbs like an eardrum at 10,000 metres.

She roasts germs from the tweezers' steel limbs with her cigarette lighter. When the handles get hot she stops the flame with a lift of thumb. Hygienic. Wiping away the soot, she picks off five minutes' worth of paper, skin and nail. Almost to the moon. Running her finger under the tap eases out a wince. 'Water take me home,' she sings, almost in key, dancing her blue toenails beneath the bathroom sink. Two of four Hollywood-style globes snap and hum.

Turning the cold tap left, she lathers up the one hotel soap cake not already in her travel bag and puts her finger in the bubbles. The sting brings a squint. The squint brings wrinkles. She holds the squint for certainty. She holds the squint to tally a census.

Fourteen. Six under the right eye and eight under the left.

The winking eye has one more wrinkle than the last time she checked. In a hotel room similar to this one, with a north-facing balcony, waiting for Campbell's Tomato Soup, she counted thirteen wrinkles. Now it's fourteen. It makes her twenty-three look twenty-three. Her winking eye deserves rest. With eyes barely visible in the bathroom mirror, she decides to not wink at Room Service Boys or pilots or dentists or judges or children anymore. Children can't wink properly anyway. Miss Lamp weathers the damage of the wink. Cut down a tree and count the rings around its drying heart. Miss Lamp lets her face drop. It's her mother's fault.

§

Half-Pint.

Young Young Miss Lamp learned to wink at age eight.

Grandma drank vinegar. Grandma yelled at Abby for using Windex and paper towels for the windows instead of old newspapers and white vinegar. Grandma belched, 'One part to two, Abby dear. One part to two. Don't use malt either, white is best.'

Sliding her bum down the wooden steps one typically sunny morning when there was no school bus to catch, Young Young Miss Lamp saw Grandma chug half a pint of white vinegar, pouring the rest in the window bucket. Stuck for words, she climbed her bum back up the well-worn stairs. Abby was making the beds, folding hospital corners, sheets still warm.

'Mom?'

'Yes, dear?' Abby pulled the sheet taut.

'How do I talk to Grandma?'

'Is she drinking vinegar again?' Abby folded over the bed covers with ample room for the pillow.

'Yes, Mom.'

'Well, wait till she's finished the windows, then wink at her.' Abby replaced the pillow, fluffing it up in one, two, three. 'She likes winks.'

Then, with one hand over the other, Abby's finger rolled out in a tremor. Malpracticed nerves.

With a furrow in her brow, Young Young Miss Lamp helped Abby pat wrinkles out of the bed. 'How?'

'How what, dear?'

'How do you do a wink?'

§

Dreaming of a White Christmas.

Abby and Grandma bitched about the wonderful Christmas snow falling beyond streaky hotel windows as Young Young Miss Lamp cut a dozen oranges with a plastic knife. She ground all twenty-four halves to and fro on a glass juicer. Happy juice. She didn't bother filtering out the pulp and seeds and bits of peel. Grandma didn't appreciate the juice.

'This tastes like shit!' Grandma slammed the glass down on the dining table so hard that a splash jumped out, hitting Young Young Miss Lamp in the left eye.

Irrepressible juice.

'I'm doing a wink, Mom ... Mom?'

'Don't listen to your grandmother, dear. She doesn't know what she's talking about. The juice is lovely, dear. Don't listen to her.' Abby feigned a sip.

Winking up at Abby, Young Young Miss Lamp coughed a little. 'You haven't tried it yet, Mom, and look! I'm winking. I think I'm winking.'

Abby's stare fixed on Grandma. A deadbolt. Locked. 'Why don't you be nice to your granddaughter?'

Grandma sucked in a wheeze. 'Why don't you be nice to Grandma? Eh? Why the hell did you haul us to Florida for Christmas in the goddamn snow?' She plodded to the sliding door and heaved it open. A blast of fresh air washed through the room, dancing tinsel on their plastic tree. Grandma scraped in some more air. 'Sunshine State, my ass! Can you believe it? Three inches, and the pool's got a cover on it.'

Tingling like a tin angel, Young Young Miss Lamp stepped close to the door, putting her toes on the mini-golf grass of the balcony. One, two snowflakes hit her forehead and rosy cheeks, three, melting in a drip down her nose. 'Ahh,' Young Young Miss

Lamp sighed as the snow fell. 'It's nice.' She stuck out her tongue to catch a flake.

Chilly Grandma spoke. 'Get in here, young lady, and put that tongue back in your mouth. You're not a dog!'

Young Young Miss Lamp held the door frame for leverage and stuck her tongue further out, confident the chocolate Lab back home did exactly the same for snowflakes. Mindful of Grandma's words, she came back in for a second or two, fingers kept just so.

Abby flinched, squinting at Grandma. 'Why don't you turn that frown around, old lady? And shut the door!'

So Grandma did.

In a whoosh Young Young Miss Lamp's heart rose to her throat as the heavy steel frame of the sliding glass door pinned one of her tiny fingers to the wall. Her face went white as a golf ball.

Snowflakes hurt to catch, she thought.

§

Rin-Tin-Tin.

Paper Boy picked a clump of peach lipstick from his hair, scraping it away on the corner of a brick wall. The bricks smelled like rain. His boots tapped down the street toward the river, the street slowly tenderized by raindrops as big as nickels. His boots creased his toes because he forgot to pick up his socks after breaking his good straight tooth. By the time he spotted the river, the snappy byline on his forehead read LO.

Under the grey arch of the bridge, Paper Boy picked up an empty tin beside a flat rock, big and round as a table. The water stung his wrists as he scooped up fresh ripples into his tin. He drank the water down to a familiar stomach ache, then searched for his Demerol to relax the cramped muscles around his brittle sternum. Pewter-tipped-walking-stick brittle.

Not in his jacket.

Not in his pants.

Upset by the smell of peach, he writhed and wrenched the zipper of his jacket to a snag. A magpie scoured the opposite bank, picking at the shiny stones. The zipper didn't give. The bottle opener that had freed the floss from his hands and feet dug well into his thigh but opened his jacket better than a zipper.

Paper Boy managed to rip the jacket down to his waist. His cold skin weaved in the breeze.

Chicken skin.

Lying down on the rocks, he wiggled and flopped the jacket to his knees, past his boots and off. The rain stopped. The laces of his boots came undone in a slip.

One. Two.

Tired pants rested on the table while he traipsed into the river.

It was as warm as June.

Paper Boy seethed in the river. A squeak and a sigh and the arch of the bridge above undulated in sheets of gold leaf. The crown of the sun shed its pink. He soaked his skin without rolling over onto his dirty stomach.

The water pulled him clean.

With raisins for fingertips, Paper Boy dried himself in the early sun. His elbows protruded dangerously, struggling up to coat-hanger shoulders. A dentist could fix my broken tooth, he thought, opening his eyes to sunbeams and his drinking tin. The bottle opener he left beside his pants had disappeared. So had his shredded jacket.

A familiar stomach ache.

On the opposite bank, the magpie still picked at shiny pebbles. Paper Boy saw letters on the big rock table. His raisins felt the freshly etched stone, smoothing chalky dust in syncopation with his heartbeat.

A wing flap.

Puffs of dust went away with his breath, revealing an arrow's point. The letters read THIS WAY. On the opposite bank grew a patch of spindle trees.

In blue underwear, Paper Boy cut across the bubbling cold river. Beyond the glimmer of wet pebbles and stones, a single dirt path wound up the slope. Tall grass and bulrushes lined the way.

Paper Boy's cheeks brushed against the trees. Robin red. On the tallest spindle tree of all, on a bold and sturdy branch, hung a jacket – well-tailored, in navy blue.

§

Breathing Is Good for You.

In Room 32, Miss Lamp's finger is a clean, cold beet. The lights in the bathroom, off. The faucet doesn't turn all the way to the right, so it hisses to her close ear. Warm porcelain. It's best to let her finger breathe. This technique is a favourite of Abby's. Mother knows best.

Miss Lamp recalls leaving the Florida snow in that rust-brown Ford Pinto, her mother at the wheel and Grandma smelling up the back seat, heading north along the grooved white concrete of Interstate 75.

A large orange bug with dragon wings popped on the windshield. A smear of red and yellow. Young Young Miss Lamp dabbed her dented finger on her purple Toughskin jeans. She had scooped up some Florida beach into her pocket before they left. A convenient band-aid.

Abby pressed knuckles to the wheel. 'Let it breathe, dear, let the finger breathe for a while – at least until we get home. And don't touch!'

'Why, Mom?'

'The air allows your finger to heal more quickly, dear. You want your finger to heal, don't you?'

Young Young Miss Lamp wasn't sure her finger could breathe. The breeze coming from the air vents was as cold as snow and her finger breathed goosebumps all up her arms.

Grandma snored to the squeak of windshield wipers.

In and out. In and out.

So Miss Lamp lets her wound breathe. Same finger.

As the sun flattens to orange, she waits for her tomato soup and grilled cheese, waits for a bold, crisp dill pickle wet in her mouth. It isn't Saturday, and she doesn't have her guitar, so she can indulge.

Miss Lamp doesn't care for grilled cheese without a dill pickle.

§

The Dog's Breakfast.
Young Young Miss Lamp's finger pressed Abby to tears. Band-aids filled up with iron, too soaked to swallow. When the ugly words were packed and zipped away for the drive back home from Florida, the nail on her index finger turned purple and fell off. It itched.

Abby cried after the nail fell off. They sat together on the squeaky porch swing while it decided to peel free. 'It's not itchy anymore, Mom.' The purple nail curved upward. A tiny dried-up leaf of a jade plant.

'Your grandma cares about you, dear.' Abby placed the nail gently in her pocket. 'I'm sorry I dented your finger. Does it hurt still?'

'No.' Young Young Miss Lamp was an exceptional liar and gave it a rub. 'But it feels funny on top, and I bet I'll have a scar.'

The porch swing kicked back as Abby went inside. Her daughter jumped at the smack of the wooden screen door. High up in the willow tree, finches chirped amongst themselves and warmed the sun to pink.

Young Young Miss Lamp touched her finger once, twice, slowly, at home below a busy cloud of gnats. She didn't have a dog, so she swung in her seat waiting for the chocolate Lab behind the whiteboard fence to chase that garbage-eating magpie through a hole large enough to fit a magpie but not a chocolate Lab. The Lab pawed and pushed its nose just above the breeze line of the fence, only to snort, sniff, howl and scratch back down the fence. The smell of magpie. A lean Christmas turkey.

'Poor stupid dog.' Young Young Miss Lamp gave him a whistle. 'I'm going to have a scar for certain.'

She glimpsed the dog through the slats of the well-flaked fence, shy a coat of white paint. The dog whimpered to a standstill with a cloud of busy gnats gathering around his chocolate Lab head. His jaw clacked in a snap.

'It's simple, dog,' she continued with a squint. 'Your masters will never let you catch that squawky magpie. That's what the hole in the fence is for. Who wants to clean up a dead bird in their backyard? Stupid dog.' The gnats parted for Young Young Miss Lamp as she rose to her feet.

The breeze was unseasonably warm.

§

Berrylicious.

       'I'm so sad,' Paper Boy said to the tallest spindle tree. Rick and Serge's lipstick letters left knuckle-sized bruises on his chest. After he slung the silk-lined suit coat on his bony shoulders, his bluish fingers picked buttons shut. Bits of dirt stuck to the fuzz on the back of his neck. Damp. His angry stomach told his hands to pick as many pink and red spindle berries as the pockets of his new jacket would hold. 'I should wash these little berries,' he said.

    The river gobbled many little berries. He watched them bob along the silver edge of current and held on to as many of the pink and red berries as he could. Trickles of purple ran down his walking muscles as silk-lined pockets strained with their dripping cargo. Returning to his drinking tin, sharp enough to catch a lip on, Paper Boy spilled the spindle berries on the table. He picked at them like Robin Redbreast. With each berry he chewed and rolled in his mouth from sweet to sour, his tongue grew numb. So did his throat. So did his angry stomach. He missed his good straight tooth.

§

Lost and Flowered.

The phone in Delano's office never rang. He had ripped the bells out of it years ago. On the elevator outside his office, down the hall, past two doors to the right, hung a sign that read OUT OF SERVICE. Abby read a sign in the lobby that said USE THE STAIRS.

Holding tight to the banister, she began her ascent. Rounding the second floor, she stooped to tie her shoe and then blew on her sweaty palms. Abby had wanted her mom to come inside and up the stairs with her. But her mom chose to scrape her heels on the sidewalk, pointing up to the busy-looking placard and clutching a note from Mr. Tall about Abby's barn-like behaviour.

'Your teacher says you've been complaining about your teeth all week, Abby. He isn't sure why. He suggests I take you to the dentist. So get up there and see what's wrong with your goddamn teeth. Third door on the left, Abby. See the sign? Hurry up.' Her mom counted on her fingers. 'One. Two. Three. Do you know which way *left* is, Abby dear? Get going! Someone has to pay for your teeth.' She mustered up some spittle. 'At least you managed to clean up your shoes, but they still smell like piss and vinegar. I want you to scrub them as soon as you get home. The poor dentist is going to have to plug his nose 'cause of those shoes. Now get going, and don't forget to stand up straight and smile. Be polite!'

With shoes wiped clean and tied tight, Abby tried to smile as she passed the second floor.

Abby was used to doing things by herself. A shoelace around her neck held a house key. It was nice and cool to touch, and Abby wore it every day. She cooked her own dinner too. Jiffy Pop hurt her teeth, though she popped it without burning a single kernel. Peanut butter and lettuce sandwiches would be easier to eat. Her mom grinned for broccoli and mushy peas with vinegar. Beans on toast and poached eggs. Abby knew just how much vinegar to put in the water. 'More than a teaspoon, less than a tablespoon, makes those eggs *swoon*,' Abby said. Abby was hungry.

Up the flight of stairs to the third floor, Abby grabbed the banister with both hands. A large woman in a chartreuse dress flew past her, throwing a pink plastic hair flower to the ground. Mascara ran down her face in streaks. She was oblivious to Abby, who picked up the flower and stretched to her tiptoes, peering over the railing down to the lobby. 'Lady, lady! You dropped your flower! Lady! Wait!'

The lady and her beautifully flowing dress of yellowish green disappeared. Abby held the flower. A pink gerbera. It smelled of hairspray. Like perfume. It had a green stem, bendy as a pipe cleaner. Abby put it in her hair and found the third floor. She turned left, three doors down. 'Excuse me, do you know where the dentist's is?' asked Abby.

A man was wiping his teeth with the back of his tie. He checked his breath in his hand and smirked. 'Why, yes I do, young lady.' He fixed his tie, adjusting the knot flat to his chest.

'Is it here?'

'It is here, and the dentist is me.'

'Oh.' Abby stood up straight and pursed her lips.

'Where's your mother, young lady? You didn't come up all these stairs by yourself, did you?' He seemed concerned.

Abby felt for the flower in her hair. 'Yes. My mom is out getting money for my teeth.'

'Teeth, eh? Well. You've come to the right place, I'm afraid.'

Abby didn't smile.

'Delano's the name. Low Rates. Satisfaction Guaranteed. No Questions Asked. What's your name then, young lady?'

'Abby Lamp.'

'That's a nice name, isn't it? Sounds shiny. Nice to meet you.' He stuck out his hand.

'I'm not supposed to shake hands with a stranger, sir.'

Delano sauntered back, ruefully aghast. '"Sir"? I'm not a stranger. I'm your dentist. A dentist is never a stranger. Ha.'

Abby sniffed at her vinegar shoes.

'Well, I suppose we should have a gander at your teeth, young lady. Come on in. Right this way. It's good and sunny in here today.'

Abby stepped into his office with a squint.

'Step right this way to the big old chair for a million-dollar smile.'

'A *million* dollars?' Abby gulped. 'My mom sure doesn't have a million dollars.'

'Oh no, young lady. Ha! That's only a figure of speech. It shouldn't cost all that much. Special rates for you, my young friend.'

Abby hopped in the big old chair.

'Sure is a nice flower you have in your hair, Abby Lamp. Pink is a wonderful colour for a girl.'

Abby smiled a little.

§

The Pickle.

The Cook rings the kitchen bell, so Room Service Boy gets off his chair. He presses wrinkles from his lap and swings through the kitchen door with his two straight cuffs. Mindful of the wet kitchen floor, he eyes The Cook.

'Is this it?'

The steam from lightly browned bread and old cheddar cheese whets Room Service Boy's appetite. The soup suspends flecks of parsley and black peppercorns. Freshly cracked. The pink hue in the blue bowl means the soup contains at least one part milk. Two thin slices of cantaloupe dignify the matching plate. Last week's honeydew melon balls would certainly have clashed.

'Where's the pickle? It needs a pickle. It's a grilled cheese. The lady in Room 32 wants a pickle with her grilled cheese.' Room Service Boy pays attention to detail.

A gravelly sigh brings the impressive jar of Bick's Polski Ogorki dill pickles down from the top shelf and onto the wooden cutting board. The Cook's stubby little fingers twist away the lid, dive into the brine and flick about for a keeper. His stubby little fingers find a shiny, well-textured specimen of deepest green. He holds it under the heat lamp, dripping shiny brine from his stubby thumb and forefinger, seeking approval from Room Service Boy.

With hands clasped together and a nod of chin to chest, Room Service Boy admires The Cook's dirt-free nails. The garlic in the brine keeps them clean. The Cook cleans a thin knife on his apron, eyeing the moist pickle on the cutting board.

Chop chop. Chop.

He places four symmetrical, aromatic pickle quarters on the blue plate, employing great care not to disturb the garnish of cantaloupe. Under the lava glow of the heat lamp, the pickle lets out a sizzle.

'Yeah. I bet she does,' says The Cook.

Room Service Boy straightens his cuffs again, noticing the shine of the heat lamp on the wet kitchen floor. He should mop it up for safety. 'Does what?'

'Wants a pickle.'

'A what?'

'A *pi-ckle.*'

The Cook unties his apron as Room Service Boy removes a plastic tray from the stack, examining it for cleanliness. He folds a clean yellow linen napkin in the shape of a triangle and places a large soup spoon in the middle of it. He pulls enough cuff to grasp blue plate, saucer and bowl away from the gnaw of the heat lamp. The food for Room 32 appears on the tray without a spilled drop or shaken crumb. Three seconds. Room Service Boy takes pride in his efficiency.

The Cook folds his greasy apron over his arm. 'Get it?' he says.

'Get what?'

With a strange gesticulation of hips, The Cook hovers those stubby little fingers around his fat white T-shirt belly and his belt. These two articles of clothing don't quite meet up over the bounty of coarse black curls hiding his belly button. In a circular motion of hands, with pelvic thrusts for emphasis, he says, 'The pickle. The pickle. The *pi-ckle.*' A bead of sweat runs down his forehead, right through a fence of hairnet.

'Oh,' Room Service Boy replies, placing the tray on the cutlery table beside the juice fridge. Quickly. One small carton of Tropicana Orange-Peach. One bendy straw, and a single plastic daisy in a single plastic daisy holder. The modest card reads FOR OUR VALUED GUEST. He never knew The Cook could dance so well.

Past the swing of the kitchen door, Room Service Boy finds a comfortable stride clear across the lobby to the elevator that works best. Balancing the tray in one arm, he tries not to smell the food too much, as it would diminish its value. The elevator goes *ding*.

'The Cook sure likes pickles,' he says to Front Desk Man.

'Thirty-two. Thirty-two!' Front Desk Man shouts.

During the twenty-three seconds it takes to arrive at the third floor, Room Service Boy ponders the value of a guest. Every day, card after card disappears from the stack on the cutlery table with the wobbly leg, beside the noisy, noisy juice fridge leaking water all over the kitchen floor. Unsafe. He should mop it up for safety. Staring at the card on the tray, he sees no candy beside it, and no wrapper that reads COURTESY MINT, because the mint is in his mouth.

The third floor dings clearer than the others. He sniffs at his armpits, catches a glance of his purple dickie bow tie, slightly askew, and prides himself on his fresh breath. 'Very important face to face,' he remarks.

Usually, he gets from the elevator door to Room 32 in eighteen generous steps. He might be able to do it in seventeen today. He is on stride. Solving the enigma of being helped out with a can of soup lessens the desire to bite his lip. Minty.

Banana Tray Hair's reference to him as Soup Boy over the entire public-address system of Safeway gives him an efficient idea. With one leg significantly longer than the other, and the special shoes she wears, Banana Tray Hair improves Room Service Boy's sixth possibility of being helped out of Safeway with a can of soup:

6. Banana Tray Hair delivers the soup to Room 32 without spilling it – in fewer than seventeen steps.

§

Smiles Are Always Free.

Miss Lamp in Room 32 receives a crisp knock at the door.

'Room service, ma'am. Room service?'

Miss Lamp doesn't enjoy waiting for her dinner on the edge of her bed.

Room Service Boy forgot to fix his cuff after picking up such absurdly hot stoneware. *Pi-ckles* have entered his mind seven times since the dance show in the kitchen.

Miss Lamp rises in her flannel pyjamas patterned with many Mounties on horseback or standing in salute. She shakes her hair in the mirror on the wall, giving it necessary tousle. The door clicks open and hushes on the carpet.

'Campbell's Tomato Soup and grilled cheese with a pickle, ma'am.' Room Service Boy grins with chalky teeth, fresh breath and a spotty face.

Miss Lamp's winking eye twitches once or twice.

'How was your flight, ma'am?' Room Service Boy wants to collect Air Miles.

Miss Lamp clears her throat. 'Did you make this soup with moomoo? Because it has to be made with moomoo.'

'Moomoo ... ? Ma'am? Do you mean – '

'Moomoo!' She says it more clearly. 'What kind of moomoo did you use? Skim moomoo? Two-percent moomoo? Homo moomoo? What kind? You didn't use powdered moomoo, did you?' She examines the soup for lumps. 'I can't eat Campbell's Tomato Soup with any old kind of moomoo.'

Thoroughly confused, he replies, 'I didn't make the soup, ma'am, The Cook did, and I'm absolutely sure he made this exact bowl of soup with no less than one part milk, um, moomoo, because it gives the soup its calcium factor, pinkish hue and nice creamy taste. In fact, I would guess the soup is made with whole moomoo, and it may be getting cold.' He stares down at the soup, steam dwindling above his cuffs.

'All right then.' Miss Lamp, with thoughtfully messy hair, flannel Mountie pyjamas and glasses for reading, continues. 'I can't have any old kind of moomoo, you know. That skim moomoo stuff is blue. Put it on the table over there, beside the chair. I think the chair is broken, by the way.'

She turns her attention to the food. 'Is the grilled cheese cut to corners? Yes. And the pickle? Good. And a bendy straw for my juice? You did use old cheddar, right?'

'Sure did, ma'am, old cheddar. Cracker Barrel. Dairy section. Aisle 8, ma'am.'

Miss Lamp hovers over her food with a sharp nose, a rabbit sniffing at a carrot that's too clean. 'Good. This will do fine.'

Room Service Boy counts fibres in the berber.

'Yes, looks quite delicious. It will do just fine.'

Miss Lamp wonders if she repeats herself.

Head down, Room Service Boy fixes his cuffs, then turns his eyes up to Miss Lamp. She removes thin glasses with green rims from her silver glasses case. Her thin glasses rest slightly above her nose as she sits on the rough wooden chair. Flannel Mounties offer slight protection from slivers. Room Service Boy reaches out his hand, turning an open palm. Head down.

'No, no, this will be more than adequate. Thank you, and please tell the front desk I wish not to be disturbed. I do have a lot of reading to do.'

Miss Lamp shakes her sandy-brown hair in the mirror and picks up the spoon from its resting place. She unfolds the yellow napkin on her lap. The spoon breaks the thin film of milk, tomato, cracked black peppercorns and fresh parsley.

Room Service Boy steps back into the hall cautiously. 'Thank you, ma'am. Um, enjoy your meal then.'

He turns his hand back to his thigh. The door sweeps shut.

Miss Lamp puts down her spoon and gives the plastic daisy a sniff. Coughing at dust, she picks up her spoon once more. Her mouth moistens to its corners.

Miss Lamp craves peaches for dessert.

§

The Polka-Dot Door.

 After the wooden porch door smacked shut, Young Young Miss Lamp listened to her mother cry in the kitchen. Looking at her cold, dirty toes, Young Young Miss Lamp wondered if Abby would cry if she had lost a toenail instead. Probably not. No one pays as much attention to toes as fingers. Except for the scab that turned green when her finger got wet in the tub, it worked fine. It pointed and scratched, poked and picked her nose as always. Young Young Miss Lamp relished the couple of weeks when she substituted other, less tender fingers for the picking. Definitely not worth crying over.

 She felt sorry for the stupid chocolate Lab losing the magpie every day. 'Magpies sure are smart,' she whispered as her wee flip-flops joined the row of runners, dress-up shoes and grandma shoes. 'Magpies can get away with whatever they like and I'm going to write a story about one,' she said.

 Young Young Miss Lamp, with gnats in her hair and dirty toes not so cold anymore, listened to stories without potatoes in her ears. Grandma told her potatoes don't belong in a young girl's ears. Before bed, Abby read her tales about stolen rings or a crooked shoe on the wrong princess's foot. She read her tales of characters with happy names like Pippi and Snoopy in places as far away as Solla Sollew. She even knew about Peach Boy, a miniature samurai born from the pit of a peach and just as tough.

 Young Young Miss Lamp loved Abby's stories, but Grandma's stories scared the hell out of her. Scared her enough to wet the bed. Grim tales about children who get eaten if they lie, children who get eaten if they tell the truth too much. Vinegar-voiced stories of dark caves, ovens, closets and dogs that won't stop barking. Grandma's song about a magpie scared her most of all. It scared potatoes up out of the earth and back into her ears.

'I'll bake you up in a pie, wee girly. I'll bake you up in a pie,' Grandma sang. 'I'll use my sharp teeth to grind your bones and bake you up in a pie. My pot is packed with children who lie. I'll bake you up in a pie.'

Grandma grew noises under the bed, made Young Young Miss Lamp see little black dots when she opened her eyes in the sunshine.

§

Mmm, Mmm, Good.

Young Young Miss Lamp leaned into the kitchen. Her dirty toes pushed into the linoleum. Abby raised her left hand high above her head. Her pointer finger shook and twitched almost an inch each way as she held her wrist tight. The magpie chattered to the window ledge. Abby didn't trust magpies. She grabbed a tea towel, wrapping her convulsing finger together with the rest of her hand, and pressed the bundle hard to her stomach. Creased in stress.

The magpie didn't flinch.

'Get away, stupid bird! Shoo! I don't have anything for you.'

The magpie didn't flinch at all.

'I have nothing for you, magpie, go away. You frightened me.'

Young Young Miss Lamp huffed. Quietly. 'Maybe he wants to help, Mom. To check if you're okay. Magpies are very smart.' She thought about Grandma's pie story and the taste of ground bones.

Abby crumpled the tea towel behind her back and dropped it in the sink. With right hand over left, she squeezed her knuckles white. A strand of red hair hung down her cheek, tickling eyelashes in front of jade-green eyes. 'When did you come in? I thought you were on the porch swing.'

'I was.'

'Are you hungry?'

'My feets was cold.' Young Young Miss Lamp covered dirty toes with more dirty toes.

'My feet *were* cold, dear, *were* cold – '

'And my toes too.'

Young Young Miss Lamp enjoyed saying words incorrectly, blinking at her mom's corrections, especially if the correct part sounded higher than it really should be. She sat up straight at the kitchen table. She giggled when the paper towel got folded into a triangle – more exciting than a square, she reckoned. Her mom always put a bit of spit on it, wiping harder than she needed to at those tomato-soup spots around the mouth and chin.

Warm as a soda cracker.

'Why were you crying, Mom?'

'Would you like grilled cheese and tomato soup?' Abby knew when her daughter was hungry.

'Golden brown. Cut in triangles. And if it's Campbell's with moomoo.' Young Young Miss Lamp stood up on her tippy-toes, peering into the cupboard with no doors.

'Yes, dear. I haven't poisoned you yet, have I?'

§

Double Your Pleasure.

Abby learned to snap and crack her Wrigley's Peppermint by watching her mom do it. She'd say, 'Like this' and 'You got it. Spread it thin on your tongue and snap till your ears ring – till your ears ring, girl.' Abby snapped and cracked her Wrigley's in a schoolroom of wooden desks and pointers.

Mr. Tall was a stern teacher with tin-rimmed glasses. His permanent forehead creases disagreed with the snapping of gum. Immediately. He told Abby to stand in the middle of the aisle. 'Since you insist on sharing your skills with the class, show us all how well you can chew your gum, young lady.'

She began to chew.

'As fast as you can. Please. We are all very impressed.' He lifted his nose and stood up from his chair, tapping a wooden pointer on his desk like a metronome. 'Faster.'

She chewed faster.

Tap tap Tap tap Tap.

The other children frowned, grinned and pointed.

Tap tap Tap tap Tap.

Abby chewed and chewed the gum to pulp, chipping enamel and snapping at the roots where her old-person teeth would grow.

The laughing of her recess friends did not stop her from crying or forming a pool of urine around her spotless black-and-white Buster Brown shoes. Mr. Tall directed his metronome to the door. With a long finger he said, 'Go to the office and get a bucket and a mop now, Abby Lamp! Do it. You clean up this disgusting mess. And you'd better learn to control yourself, young lady – this is not a barn!'

She tried to glint at the smirks of her classmates, but her teeth wouldn't let her. She had had such fun playing hopscotch that she had forgotten to go to the bathroom before the end of recess.

She did, however, stock up with a fresh piece of Wrigley's after using up a whole piece showing how to crack gum and blow bubbles without getting it caught in your pigtails. The squeak of her damp Buster Browns down the corridor jarred her molars. The classroom smelled of vinegar all week. Whenever Mr. Tall shouted, 'Someone please open a window in here,' Abby's teeth hurt.

§

She Has the Freshest Mouth in Town.

Miss Lamp sips on her carton of juice. Pushing the bendy straw to one side, she wipes tomato soup from the corners of her mouth with yellow linen. The pickle quarters complemented her last gulp of soup exquisitely. Parsley, pepper and a twist of dill. Room Service Boy hadn't asked her for a tip. She keeps spare change handy for Room Service Boys.

Picking at the plastic daisy in the plastic daisy holder reminds her of composite teeth. 'They last forever,' she remarks. Her laptop clicks, whirrs and beeps a few times, glowing an eventual somnambulant blue. Adjusting her bum, she's concerned for the flannel Mounties guarding her skin against slivers. 'Such an uneasy chair,' she sighs. 'They can't protect me now.' Crunching a piece of Dentyne Ice Midnight Mint into her mouth, she inhales a blast of menthol. 'Ooh. This is strong.'

The manila envelope marked DELANO lies fat on the freshly made bed. Careful of her sliced beet, Miss Lamp peels the sticky tab back gently so as not to rip the envelope or its contents or another one of her fingers, stopping only to keep her green-rimmed glasses from falling off her nose. The papers expand as she places them on the table.

They feel humid.

§

Lip Service.

Paper Boy twitched like a fish hooked through the gills. He shook on the spot and the spot rattled. He tugged on his fancy jacket and the rattle got louder. His lips tasted spindle-berry numb. 'Ah my wibs bwoken too?' His lips fat on spindle-berry juice. 'Whas in ma pawkit?'

He undid the top two buttons of his new suit jacket and felt inside. Wavering thin as a whippet in the eye-high sun, he found a screw-top attached to an orange plastic pill bottle. The label suggested TAKE THESE WITH FOOD. As he had some berries in his mouth, and several in his belly, he swallowed two purple Demerol tablets to relax the tight lines of his chest.

On his way up the hill, he sniffed at the baking of bread. He met people going to work, people rattling garbage-can lids and people shouting the facts of the day from newspaper stands. Scratching bits of twigs and mud from his hair, he supposed his jacket looked nice. Sharp.

A real Robin Redbreast.

Passersby aplenty noted the fine cut of his jib and murmured, 'Has that young fella been out to sea? Look at that stride! And such seaworthy legs! Oh, how his black boots shine in the light of day. Make way. Make way!' The jacket really was exceptional – silk on the inside and navy-blue polyester, for show. He had never been on any kind of boat, let alone set out to sea.

He shook his head and whistled to a stop below a busy-looking placard hanging from large brass hooks, three floors up. His lips helped him read properly.

DENTIST. INSURANCE NOT A PROBLEM. SURGERY ON
PREMISES. CASH DISCOUNTS. ORTHODONTIA.

DENTURES. HAVE A COSMETIC SMILE. NO QUESTIONS
ASKED. COMPLETE CONFIDENTIALITY AND COMFORT.
THIRD FLOOR. DOOR ON LEFT.

Paper Boy gawked up at the two-tone sign, sucking at the remainder of his good straight tooth. His knees buckled like anchor chains and his head hit the curb in a heap. Sharp. The passersby aplenty did not say a word.

§

The Egg.

Young Young Miss Lamp scrambled into position, sitting on her knees, straightening up her back for each scratch.

'You missed a spot, Mom ... To the left ... No, left ... Up, ahhh.'

Abby squeezed a loose fist in the shape of an egg and tapped out a crack. Her thin fingers danced down her daughter's sandy-brown hair.

'The egg! Can you do a two-handed egg, Mom?'

'You've got a bit of a sunburn – you have more freckles every summer.'

Finger yolk trickled down spotted shoulders, slowing to touch each freckle.

Abby spoke again. 'Don't let that magpie tease you with his tail feathers of blue and green, don't mind him. He struts and picks at shiny things.'

The yolk ran down Young Young Miss Lamp's spine, sticking to the sides of her ribs, tending to a trail of goosebumps, an army of ants in tow.

Young Young Miss Lamp shivered for a second and counted ten.

'He doesn't tease me, and you shouldn't yell at him.' She wiggled on her knees. 'Do magpies eat ants, Mom?'

'Don't sit like that. Do you want to walk like a pigeon?'

§

The Craneal Nerve.

'Now, why did you do that?' Delano bent at the knees to get a better view. The downside of Paper Boy was pale and blue. A lazy ditto of himself. 'Come on, boy.'

Gathering pedestrians craned their necks into the ears of others. The passersby aplenty kept up the morning rush. A shift of paper. A scrape of heel. Blood blotted in Paper Boy's ear, and he had a nasty cut on his cheek to boot.

Delano scooped his hands under Paper Boy's coat-hanger shoulders. Delano smelled of Listerine and hand soap. Ivory. Ninety-nine and four one-hundredths pure.

Paper Boy wanted to open his eyes to morning, but his lids wouldn't flutter.

'Someone should call an ambulance, don't you think?' one crane said to another. 'I mean, it is entirely awful seeing a young boy face down and bleeding all over a perfectly good sidewalk. How is a person supposed to concentrate on getting to work? It saddens the morning sun, don't you think? Where is his mother, for heaven's sake?'

The other crane nodded. 'Yes. Yes, I think he does require an ambulance. He's certainly not moving much.'

'He's not moving.'

'Absolutely.'

One crane turned past the other, squinting toward the clock tower. The clock tower had a clock as big as a barn, with big hands moving when and where they should.

'What time does it say?'

'You mean you can't tell from here?'

'I – I don't have my glasses with me this morning. I seem to have forgotten them.'

'Maybe on the train?'

'Maybe.'

'You were reading on the train, weren't you?'

'I was. But I don't need them for reading.'

The two cranes stood spitting distance from the crumpled Paper Boy with no mother, pale and blue on the sidewalk. At ten to nine the morning crowd thinned out.

One crane cooed, 'Do we have time to call for an ambulance before work?'

'No. No, I believe not. Not unless you hope to be late,' cooed the other.

'Where is his mother? Such a shame, and so well-dressed. Come now.'

'I suppose that man is caring for him, isn't he.'

'Yes. Yes, I believe he is. Absolutely.'

With a tug of arms and a clack of heels, the cranes disappeared.

§

Music Box Dancers.

The overhanging lamp that Miss Lamp bumps her head on is not shiny enough to read by, so she plugs in her handy portable reading lamp instead. It buzzes and beams through a tint of green glass. The manila of the empty DELANO envelope complements the Indian-red leather of her litigation bag.

Miss Lamp imagines Abby under the well-focused light, her pale green eyes. Miss Lamp's litigation bag holds a music box of cherrywood for Abby. The music box churns more than one Patsy Cline song – more than 'Crazy.' With a twist of a key, it becomes a dusty saloon player piano with nine working keys. Miss Lamp sees Abby dance to the lilt of the music box, threading its spindle of warm rubber-band notes.

Young Young Miss Lamp learned to turn her mom properly by the second verse without trampling on her toes by the third.

Miss Lamp prefers to lead.

Tall sunflowers grow next to Abby's mailbox.

§

Polish Those Pearly Whites.

'Come on, boy, you have to stop bleeding in front of my office. It's not the best for business.' Delano retrieved a paper tube of sniffing salts from his maroon jacket. In a snap he said, 'This usually works for me. Breathe it in. *Breathe.*'

Paper Boy coughed up a mouthful. 'I need a dentitht. I need a dentitht now.'

Delano rose to his feet in exclamation. 'Did you say a *dentist*, boy? Why, that's who I am. You've come to the right place, I'm afraid.' He yanked his green silk tie to his Adam's apple. Taut. 'Insurance? Not a problem! Cash discounts? Why not! Step on in. Guaranteed comfort allows for all the latest equipment. Ah ... yes. You could use a hand there, young man. Right this way. Third floor. Door on your left, remember, left.' Delano held a long blink. 'You did say you needed a dentist, right, boy?'

'I need a dentitht.'

Delano turned to the thinning crowd of cranes and passersby aplenty. 'Don't want to be late for work now, do we? The boy's fine. It's only blood, only a little blood. There's nothing to see here – move along now.' His fingers flipped direction from flicking the crowd away to poking his own barrel chest. 'This boy will have the smile of an angel to grace our fine sidewalks. Of an angel. Affordable rates. No questions asked. Complete confidentiality guaranteed.' Delano's beak flapped like a placard.

His meat hooks pulled Paper Boy along. Paper Boy didn't mind being dragged up the six flights of wooden stairs to the third floor, door on left.

Demerol kept his body asleep.

On the way up the stairs, Delano blurted, 'Just my luck. The elevator's been broken for weeks. It's a good thing you're not much more than a couple sacks of potatoes.' He huffed at the dead weight, the lines of his pumpkin forehead forging beads of sweat. 'Did you eat a durian this morning, junior? You smell funny.' Delano avoided fruit at every port.

He rested Paper Boy against the hallway wall, fumbled for his keys and clicked open the door to a musty, broken room. 'Ahh, yes, as it was, as it was.' He cracked open the wooden blinds to let sun on dust. Delano had painted the windows shut years ago.

No room for air, or for ether either.

'Oh, look! I've left you in the hall. What kind of dentist would I be if I left you slumped over in the hall all morning?' Delano dusted off the big old chair with his tie, slipped Paper Boy into the pocket of the big old chair, shut the door and latched the lock. 'Your teeth, is it? Yes. Usually the case.' He paused and touched his fingertip to the pus running the length of Paper Boy's jaw. 'What happened to your face?'

Sticky as glue.

Delano strapped on his forehead mirror, then manoeuvred a dusty steel tray with wheels to his side. A tall glass jar of cotton balls stood next to a plastic bottle of rubbing alcohol. The label read NOT FOR DRINKING. Steel picks and prods, some with mirrors on their ends, lay folded in a dirty white towel. Long cotton swabs, wooden tongue depressors, dental floss, small glass jars with tinfoil lids, an array of needles, tweezers and clamps all placed next to an ashtray full of silver amalgam. The drill rested on a table of its own.

A cotton ball soaked in rubbing alcohol wrinkled Paper Boy's cheek. 'I don't think you'll need stitches. Hmm. Hold your head still now.'

Paper Boy fixed on a circular reflection of himself. Shaky.

'Can you open your mouth? Good. A little wider. Um. Hmm. As I suspected. Incisor, is it? Not much left there.'

Delano got a small flashlight from the steel table, turned it on and held it with his teeth. Then he unfolded the dirty white towel and picked out a shiny descaler. The flashlight toned down his voice. 'Ah, yes. There's the nerve, all right. Not good.' He pried the back of half a good straight tooth. 'Can you feel that?'

Paper Boy quivered in the big old chair as Delano pressed Paper Boy's shoulder with his hands.

'I'll give you a needle, boy, you won't feel a thing. Guaranteed comfort.' He flicked at a small bottle with a tinfoil cap, found an empty syringe and proceeded to fill it. Tapping out tiny air bubbles, he said, 'This might pinch a little. It's a new thing we call freezing.' He jammed the needle far beyond the palate of Paper Boy's mouth.

Paper Boy swivelled his head and wheezed. His shoulder throbbed. The same shoulder for years. His chest clenched tight enough to crack ribs. Next to an old grey London Fog overcoat on a brass hook was the very same pewter-tipped walking stick.

Delano attended to the drill at once. 'No time to waste. I'll just adjust the bit ... This thing's a *bit* rusty. Get it? Ha!'

Delano laughs at his own jokes.

'Don't mind the squeak. The cord of the drill connects to my foot pedal, see? The faster I push, the faster it goes. Once I push fast enough, it's like electricity. Just like it. You'd think we could get some juice in this place. Now hold still and open up. Perfect. The sunlight is per–'

Paper Boy gagged as the filing drill bit caught his lip. Whirr. Spatters of his blood speckled Delano's sweaty forehead, and mirror.

'Sorry about that. Not fast enough.' Delano lifted his knee. 'Have you heard any funny jokes lately?' The pump of his foot shook the floor. 'She's spinnin' now.'

Paper Boy hoped the burnt-flesh smell would go away.

'Well, junior, the little bastard's going to have to come out. Can't fix it. Can't cap it. No nerve left. It will probably end up turning grey then black and falling out anyway. You don't want that. A man as young as yourself should look his best at all times, especially for the ladies. I'll simply locate my pliers and we'll be ready to – ' Paper Boy shut his own blinds. 'Are you all right, Paper Boy? You remembered my newspaper, didn't you? The river was a little cold this morning, wasn't it? But the jacket fits well – a tad loose in the shoulders, but good.'

'What are you going to do to me?'

'The tooth has got to go, but I'll set you up with a nice gold one. Low rates. The ladies like 'em. Remember that.'

Delano found his yellow-handled pliers on the window ledge, scratched his head and adjusted the elastic of his forehead mirror. He put his knee to Paper Boy's brittle chest, grasping the tooth with pincers and a tug.

'This might pinch a little,' he said.

§

Lay Off of My Red Suede Shoes.
Young Miss Lamp left the hotel room before the sun hit eleven o'clock. She freed her toes from the knotted sheets of the bed. She zipped her yellow party dress alluringly to her back while Rick and Serge snored soundly on their backs in a miasma of sour rum and ashtrays. She winced at their well-covered toes and shook her hair in a whisper. 'I don't get how you guys can sleep. It's ludicrous. Sweaty toes are bad news.'

Her well-plucked eyebrows raised themselves to the day without a crinkle. Her hair didn't hurt either.

Supple roots.

It smelled of fresh lemons and watermelons, as sparky as when she got Rick and Serge to buy her a twenty-sixer of Captain Morgan. Spicy. She pushed past the wooden chair to the bathroom, finding her red purse sideways but well-contained. Some string attached itself to her turquoise toenails.

The miniature tiles of the bathroom floor cooled the soles of her temperate feet. 'Ahhh,' she moaned, 'that's good times.'

After giving her face a splash and a wipe with a starchy washcloth far too small for washing, Young Miss Lamp reached for a towel. 'What's a T-shirt doing here?' she whispered, wiping eyes on her arm.

Her subtle cream-and-pinkish hue turned to a stop sign as she leaned into the tub. 'Where is he anyway? I haven't seen him since he was asleep on the chair.'

Twisting rusty drips into the drain, her delicate, smoky fingers put the shirt in her purse. Queasy. Young Miss Lamp did not remember writing the word DIRTY on Paper Boy's belly.

Closing her purse, she marched away without saying goodbye and without her shoes. By the time the room door clicked shut, Young Miss Lamp had trounced her feet all the way to the elevator.

The force of her own breeze cooled her face a little. A subtle yield. The Coca-Cola-and-Captain-Morgan stain just below her belly button shamed her face warm again. The dress was new three days ago and she hadn't even modelled it for her mother yet. Yellow was Abby's favourite colour too, but she couldn't drink Coca-Cola. Too hard on the teeth. 'Great. I bet that's going to stain,' Young Miss Lamp said to her dress.

A school chum of hers in Grade 6 put a tooth in a half-full can of Coke before going to bed. In the morning the Coke was still on the bookshelf, but the tooth was gone. Young Miss Lamp tongued the fuzz of overnight teeth. Her feet were itchy. 'Where are my goddamn shoes?'

During the walk back to the door, she didn't notice the smile Cleaning Lady gave her. She did notice the creases on her tired face, the curlers in her wilty hair and the hump in her back as she shoved armfuls of sweaty, twisted sheets in the canvas side pouch of the cleaning trolley. Young Miss Lamp knocked on the door in two loud sets of five. Cleanly. After hearing a mumbled 'Go away,' she repeated her assault.

'It's me – I forgot my shoes.'

Rick staggered to his feet, sporting a pair of tired lime-green underwear. The door clicked ajar. Young Miss Lamp crossed her arms.

'Why are you in the hallway?'

'I forgot my shoes.'

'Oh.'

The door swung shut. Good and locked. Young Miss Lamp made a fist and rapped on the door. Her knuckles began to smart, so she tried her best megaphone impression. 'Give me my shoes! Let me in, or get my shoes.'

'What do they look like?'

Rick had a hard time letting the light in.

'The red ones. Right there.'

'Where?'

'Right there, the suede ones.'

'Oh.'

'Never mind. I'll get them myself.'

Pushing past the smell of boy, she grabbed one, then two, of her red suede shoes, which matched her purse without a clash and brushed up rather nicely. It's not as though Rick appreciated colour coordination, in his rotting underwear, or what goes with what or why this goes with that. Young Miss Lamp ended up coordinating for mirrors mostly – for posterity's sake – proving red and yellow did go together, absolutely.

'You should come for breakfast with us. We're goin' to the Husky House. Mmm.'

Young Miss Lamp leered at the scratching of a belly. Dirty boy. 'Where is he? I found his shirt in the tub and there's string all over the floor. What did you guys do to him?'

'Bacon-and-eggs time?'

Young Miss Lamp did not disappoint her bleary-eyed observer. Red suede shoes fit snugly under her cleanly shaven armpits. Immaculate. The swing of her purse, her confident strut tapping atop the itchy carpet. She was lovely in that yellow party dress – the way her ankles turned, the flex of her strong, smooth calves right up to the lilt of her dress. Cleaning Lady smiled twice more, pushing a sheet to her face as though it were Young Miss Lamp's skin. Waiting for the elevator with her, she pressed her lips together wet to the sheet. She tasted mangoes, ripe pears and nectarines in a bloom of citrus. Cleaning Lady breathed in the sheet, breathed in until the elevator doors closed and the fruit disappeared.

§

In the White Room.

At a narrow table in a small white room with a small white door, Abby sat speechless.

The man in the chair opposite her sat extraordinarily straight in his white coat. 'Speak into the microphone, please. Let's begin. This machine tends to squeak. Sorry.' He leaned over his clipboard to press play and record simultaneously. 'Tuesday, January 8th, 9:37 in the morning. Dr. Steeves, questioning physician. Speak into the microphone clearly, please. State your given name and date of birth.'

Moving forward in her chair so as to speak into the microphone, please, Abby enunciated her words.

'My full name is Abigail Nell Grace Eunice Lamp. I go by Abby. I was born January 8th – '

'Well then, happy birthday, Abby.' Dr. Steeves's eyes matched his aura. Light blue. 'So, Abby, please tell us – '

Abby blushed, checking her posture. 'Thank you, doctor.' What nice eyes he had. Periwinkle blue. The colour of forget-me-nots. She curled up a half smile, leaning forward.

Dr. Steeves referred back to his clipboard. It smelled of damp sawdust. 'You're welcome. It's always nice to have a birthday.'

'Is it?' Her half smile held her finger in check.

'Well, I think so. They only come every so often, you know. In my profession I meet a lot of people who have birthdays.'

Abby's smile dropped.

Dr. Steeves picked up his pen and checked his list. Abby picked at the edge of the brown plastic table veneer. She didn't see a ring on his finger. 'It's just another day, don't you think?'

'Well, no. I don't think so. Some people do, I suppose, but no, I think it's a time to pause and celebrate life with people who are important to you. It's not just another day, or people would be walking around saying "Happy Tuesday" or "Have a happy Friday." It's about the meaning of "Happy Birthday." It's not "Sad Birthday" or "Banal Birthday" or "Dysfunctional Birthday." And if you've recently met the person, like you and I, for example, one uses the greeting – or phrase, I suppose – of "Happy Birthday" to reify the importance of birthday, of being born, of life itself.'

Yikes, Abby thought. This guy didn't get out much, using words like 'reify.' 'Thank you, doctor, I'm much better now. Perhaps it is more than just another day.'

Her smile returned. Almost a show of teeth. She had to remind herself she was in a small closed room with a small closed door, perched in a chair next to a narrow table with two microphones and a squeaky cassette recorder. The doctor across the table had eyes of azure, no wedding ring and a large vocabulary.

Her finger didn't move a muscle.

Dr. Steeves continued. 'Right. Can you please tell me when you first noticed a change in the behaviour of your left index finger?'

'Approximately fifteen years ago.'

'And can you describe the sensations associated with this change in your finger's behaviour?'

'Well, as I've said before – ' Abby brushed a strawberry curl from an eyelash, behaving her left hand for the calming doctor. ' – this finger moves on its own and stops on its own. I can't control it if it starts to twitch. I have to wait until it stops to think clearly again. It's electricity. Like an electrode or something gives it a whack of volts whenever I get upset. It fills up with a burn, like lactic acid. It's sore all the time. Aspirin, Tylenol, they do nothing. Muscle relaxants, Demerol or Valium, put me to sleep. I've had my girl and her grandmother to care for.'

'So you've learned to cope with your new physical condition then?' His pen moved along at a scribble's pace.

'Yes, but it's not a condition. It's me. Is this interview going to make the shaking go away? Is this going to improve with time?'

'Pardon me, Abby. You've described these paroxysms similarly before, like a whack of volts, as you say. To clarify then, for the record, there is no history of neurological disorders in your family?' Dr. Steeves wet the tip of a ballpoint pen on his tongue.

Abby noticed a stain there. A bruise on his tongue from asking too many stupid questions. She crossed her arms and leaned back in the sturdy chair. 'No.'

'No multiple sclerosis, Parkinson's, Lou Gehrig's disease?'

Her chin moved toward her chest. 'No.'

'I'm sorry, Abby. I don't believe our tape-recording machine caught your last answer clearly. Again – ' He wet his pen once more, poised to check his list. ' – your family does not have a history of neurological disorders?'

'Yes.'

The working Miss Lamp in Room 32 turns over a page of her mother's transcript. There's no mention of Delano.

§

Work Union, Live Better.

Banana Tray Hair has a natural smile. A true smiler's curvature. Subtle, without ever being too thin or too pronounced. A real soup spoon. It draws Room Service Boy away from his running tally of Safeway products, their placement in the system of numbered, fluorescent aisles and the larger socio-political implications of such products, numbers and aisles. She's tall and thin, with swizzle-stick dimensions and blond waves of hair. She could pass for a nice umbrella. She's as tall as a guard on a high school basketball team. Her special shoes keep her above the eye level of most of her valued customers. Room Service Boy's eyes meet her natural pearly whites. Her view teeters clear over the thinning curls atop the crown of his egg-shaped head.

Room Service Boy never comes through her checkout with more than ten items. Never eleven. Never fourteen. Most people try to push it. Banana Tray Hair catches them every day. People don't count their items correctly. Four oranges count as four items – not one magical group item of four oranges. Seven loaves of Flax-Seed Oat and Honey Nature Bread count as seven items. Size is irrelevant. A twenty-four jumbo-roll pack of toilet paper equals one tiny packet of Sesame Snaps. Banana Tray Hair knows her customers. Knows how they act. Don't fuck with the sign, she thinks. She blames the increase in item scanning, handling and bagging on the introduction of new shopper-friendly baskets. Twice the product in the same trip. She warned the middle-management people about this at the second annual meeting of Unionized Safeway Workers.

'These larger basket loads will simply irritate the express cashier,' said one employee.

'Then perhaps we should change the sign,' suggested another.

Don't fuck with the sign, Banana Tray Hair thought, so she spoke.

'You could change the sign, but then you'd be confusing the customer. The current baskets are in the realm of ten items. Ten items. Ten fingers. Ten means express. If you put up a sign encouraging TWENTY-FIVE ITEMS OR LESS – which is what these new babies can handle – let me tell you, it will give the customer too much mental strain, not to mention tennis elbow. How long does it take to count to twenty-five?'

As many pairs of lips began to move, Banana Tray Hair interjected with vigour. 'Well? Anyone? That's right. It takes too long and that's not express. It's math class. Do you want math class in Safeway?'

Many managers signified no thank you. One of the heads opened up its counting lips very wide to say, 'There's already enough math in our store. We certainly don't need math class. Jeez, I learnt that in Grade 8.'

'See?' Banana Tray Hair opened her arms wide, swinging her hair to and fro. 'Nobody wants to think too much in Safeway. They want things to move smoothly and quickly. I couldn't care less about the baskets – there's nothing we can do about them anyway. Progress is progress, right? Just don't – don't mess with the sign.'

Three of her express co-workers let out a hiss of air sounding like 'yessss,' followed by a faint golf clap.

'Lu-cy, Lu-cy, Lu-cy,' they chanted as she took a bow, swinging her hair fro and to. The most middle looking of the non-union management people rose to his feet. He was the emcee.

'Thank you, um, uh … ' He didn't have the necessary vision for name tags.

'Lucy.'

'Yes. Lucy. We will certainly take your comments into consideration. You have very nice hair. Now, please sit down.'

§

Banana Splints.

'Heel and toe, heel and toe.' No matter how hard Young Young Miss Lamp tried to tighten those calves, her toe would hit the ground first. 'That's why you trip, dear. It has to be heel then toe.' It frustrated Abby that the toes of her daughter's boots and shoes wore out so quickly for such a young girl. Socks right through the rubber. Toes right through the socks.

'And stop sitting on your knees,' Abby said when not too busy to look. Young Young Miss Lamp might turn into a pigeon. 'It will make you toe in, sunshine.'

Young Young Miss Lamp marvelled at the frayed fabric of her purple Toughskin jeans, the white threads tickling her kneecaps. The plaid iron-on patches were easy to pick off.

Abby was running out of patches. She decided to take her little pigeon of a daughter to the leg doctor.

The physiotherapist, gripping Abby's hand like a pencil, had said, while Young Young Miss Lamp was well within earshot, 'If she doesn't sleep with them on, she has to wear them during the day. At least six hours in the day. Eight if possible. If she wears them at night, she can play normally during the day.'

He looked down at her sandy pigtails. He handed over a pair of special sleeping shoes. Young Young Miss Lamp looked up at a rubber hammer leaning out of a big blue pocket.

'Your hammer's going to fall out,' she said.

'Does she start kindergarten this September?'

Abby nodded, squeezing her daughter's hand like a tea towel.

'I go to dinosauri school and I – '

'Montessori school, dear.'

' – and I learn French.'

'We want those feet to be straight for school, don't we?'

Abby nodded once more. The physiotherapist lifted his gaze. If Young Young Miss Lamp stared at the buzzing ceiling lights long enough, she saw a rainbow of spots behind her eyes. It was very white in there. It smelled of tape.

The physiotherapist inhaled through his nose, dimming the light in the room. 'Otherwise, her bones won't grow properly, and she will toe in permanently. It's in the hips. So make sure you put them on for her before bedtime. Nice and tight.'

He pressed a tiny button on his wristwatch and red numbers glowed in its window.

'Can she tie her shoes?'

'She's learning.' Abby's finger began to tingle.

'Don't worry, she'll get used to them. Nighttime is best. Eight hours. Nice and tight. I must be running along.' A very shiny wristwatch he had. 'I have another appointment.' He flipped through the pages of a little black book. 'You can come back for another visit in six weeks. Go see the girl up front. Have a fine day, Madame et Mademoiselle.'

The rubber hammer didn't fall out of his pocket.

§

The Early Bird.

Young Young Miss Lamp pretended to sleep. Some mornings she pretended better than others. Grandma scared her. Grandma's rough voice reeked of vinegar. Young Young Miss Lamp smelled Grandma's acrid hands, cracked and clutching the bedclothes. Bleached white.

In a hunch, Grandma barked, 'There's nothing wrong with you. It's time for you to get up.' Grandma tightened her clutch, peeling the covers off the bed. Young Young Miss Lamp pretended to sleep on her back, her grapefruit cheeks turning pink beneath brown eyes stuck shut. 'Get up, you!' As the pretender tried to shift onto her side, Grandma noticed. 'For Christ's sake! Young ladies don't sleep in their shoes.'

'They're special shoes, Grandma,' Young Young Miss Lamp said as she unglued her eyes. 'To help me walk proper for school.'

Grandma sneered toward the bed. 'Special shoes. There's nothing wrong with you. Come on. Get up! Get up! Show me you can walk properly. Special shoes. What crap. Hurry up. Show me.'

Young Young Miss Lamp wiggled herself along the bed. She straightened up her back, pushing and pulling along in stripey purple-and-white pyjamas. Abby had cut the feet out of the bottoms to accommodate the shoes for sleeping in. Young Young Miss Lamp's hands left the edge of the bed to scratch grains of sleep from her tired brown eyes. 'It's hard to move around in these shoes, Grandma. They pain.'

'So get up and walk then.' Grandma let out a cough. Bitter. It sounded the same as that rust-brown Ford Pinto in the driveway. 'Today, girl. I don't have all day. Grandma's got some windows to wash.'

She squinted her eyes to a point, fixed upon the Denis Brown Splints once more, confused at the slight shine between the feet of the young girl with the runny nose. 'Where's all the glimmer coming from? Is that a lamp at your feet?'

'It's a bar. It holds my feet together. One of them at ten o'clock and the other one at two o'clock. That's what the leg doctor says. That's what Mom says.'

'Leg doctor?'

'It pains my legs if I sleep on my tummy so I have to sleep on my back.' Knocking her shoes against the side of the bed, she almost swung to the floor.

Grandma's face wrinkled some more.

'I can almost touch, Grandma, look!'

'There's a bar on the bottom of your shoes?'

'Look, Grandma, look!'

The old woman wilted. Her knees cracked as she reached out her hands. The bar confused Grandma, all hunched down, crunching her knees into the new bedroom carpet. Sunflower yellow. Abby had laid the carpet to hide scratches on the pine-board floor. Sunflower yellow was Young Young Miss Lamp's favourite colour.

Grandma put her nose right up to the shiny bar and began to sniff.

Grandma grabbed the bar with both hands.

'Let me have that goddamn thing!' Perhaps the best way to have the goddamn thing was for her to pull on it as hard as she could. The bar and its patron slammed to the bedroom floor in a heap. Young Young Miss Lamp couldn't hold on to the fitted bottom sheet. The back of her head hit the side of the box spring. She landed smack on her tailbone.

Abby shopped for groceries while Grandma fought with the shoes. The old woman who was dragging Young Young Miss Lamp across hot, sharp, plastic carpet fibres had to eat healthily at suppertime. Had to have it cooked for her too. Had to have broccoli boiled for no longer than a minute. Otherwise, it'd be fit for the trash.

'Not even fit for the mangy mutt next door,' Grandma said. 'Is it too difficult for you, Abby, to cook something for a minute? Shall I count to sixty for you? Eh? A minute. Obviously, you forgot how to count.'

Abby poked at cinnamon buns and checked the expiry dates of skim-milk cartons and Young Young Miss Lamp screamed. She tried to stop the moving carpet with her fingernails. It was too hot. Hot sunflower seeds under her nails.

Coughing and choking through her runny nose, Young Young Miss Lamp felt tears etch red lines down her pink-grapefruit cheeks. Grandma marched circles around the room, pulling her up to speed. The carpet was too hot with those hot sunflower seeds burrowing under her nails.

'You don't need carnival shoes, dear. Let Grandma pull them off your pretty wee feet. They don't do nothin'. Show me you can walk properly once I pull them off and – '

'Stop! Stop! It pains, Grandma. Let me go! Stop! My back is burning. Mom! Help!'

'Your mother should have helped you in the first place and you wouldn't have these stupid things. I think they're getting looser. Almost got 'em. Never you mind.'

Abby had tied the shoes nice and tight. Physiotherapist's orders.

Grandma wondered why those shoes didn't just slip off. She dropped the shiny bar, and its shoes, attached by four screws in each sole, to the floor. 'Stop your crying and walk.'

Young Young Miss Lamp's feet stopped at ten o'clock and two o'clock. Exactly. Wishing those shoes would just slip off, she wiped her runny nose. Her purple-and-white-striped pyjama top stuck to her back. Wet and red.

§

How 'Bout Them Apples?

Paper Boy left the comfort of Delano's third-floor dentist office with a gold tooth in his mouth and the sun in his eyes. The sun shone well next to the clock tower. The clock was as big as a barn.

He asked the pockets of his navy-blue blazer and pants, 'Well, where am I going to get seventy dollars?' They didn't answer.

Turning to a passerby, he asked again, 'Where am I going to get seventy dollars?' The passerby didn't answer either.

The air smelled of lunchtime. People in suits rustled brown paper bags, tapping the sidewalk with their steely-tipped umbrellas as they walked past Paper Boy's gaping mouth. His teeth were dirty. He asked, 'Where am I going to get seventy dollars?'

'Pardon?' An umbrella stopped tapping.

'Where am I going to get seventy dollars?' Paper Boy didn't want to ask again.

'Seventy dollars?' asked a man smelling of Montreal smoked meat. He wore the apparel of a busy man. A suit of green tweed. He looked at his calculator-watch three times in twelve seconds.

Paper Boy counted.

'Seventy dollars for what? Are you in some kind of trouble?' Busy Man hooked his yellow umbrella on his forearm before uncrinkling his brown paper lunchtime bag. 'Do you want some food? I've got some left here ... uh, half a sandwich, a pickle, an apple. The wife always packs me an apple, can't stand 'em myself. Red, green or yellow, doesn't matter. They turn my stomach. Maybe it's the skin?' Busy Man scratched at his red beard. 'Sprayed and waxed with all that garbage. I usually give 'em away every day anyway. You could use an apple.'

The large and shiny apple rested well in Busy Man's hand. Paper Boy's new tooth was still numb.

Busy Man said, 'Here. Take it. Go on and eat something – you're quite thin indeed.' He glanced at his calculator once more, for the fourth time in thirty-two seconds. Not less.

Paper Boy counted.

Busy Man scratched at his red beard again and continued. 'Have you been out to sea or something?' He let out a warm laugh. 'I mean, with your navy sailor's jacket and your polished black leather boots there.' He inspected Paper Boy up and down. 'I've always fancied myself to be a sailor, all that adventure and what have you. Too bad we don't have a sea. I was in a city with a Naval Museum once, but no sea. I don't get it.'

Paper Boy's teeth felt as if they'd all been pushed together. 'Where am I going to get seventy dollars?' He tried to focus.

Fuzzy Busy Man put the apple back in the brown paper lunchtime bag. 'Take my lunch bag. The sandwich has meat in it. Smoked meat on rye with mustard. You have a vegetarian appearance to you. Hitler was a vegetarian – read all about it at the Naval Museum. He knew which of our boats shipped meat and sunk them too. Remember that now. Meat is good, and you're a little pale. You do eat meat, don't you?'

'Montreal smoked meat?'

'Indeed.'

Paper Boy welcomed the lunch in his hands. 'I need seventy dollars, please.'

'I'm afraid I can't help you there, son.'

In the time it took Busy Man to peruse a healthy-looking leather wallet, Paper Boy's fingers began to ache under the strain of such a meaty lunch.

'Why do you need all that cash?' Busy Man lowered his brow. 'You're not into drugs or anything, are you? I've heard about drugs on ships. Do you sailors do that sort of thing?' He showed most of a grin above a chin of burgundy bristles. 'I've needed seventy bucks now and again myself, but I can only help you out with five today.'

'Five?'

'Yup. A thin blue five. I wish I could help more, my young friend. Now go and get yourself something warm to drink.'

'Thank you, sir. Do you know where I could get sixty-five dollars?'

'I'm sure sorry I don't, son.' Busy Man rummaged through his pockets. 'What did you say the money was for, exactly?'

Paper Boy moved his tongue gingerly, crinkling his lips open, but not too wide. 'My tooth.' It hurt his lips to say 'oooh.'

Busy Man tapped his yellow umbrella to the concrete in reply. 'Your tooth? Is there a problem with your tooth? A young sailor like you shouldn't have any problems with a tooth.'

Paper Boy's face pressed into colour. A warm flash. 'It's solid gold and I have to pay for it.'

Busy Man smiled with all his teeth at once. One of the front ones shone particularly well in the overhead sun next to the clock tower. 'Me too, but the gold's too soft. That's why I don't eat apples. But the wife sure fancies the tooth.'

§

Skin Deep.

It frustrates Miss Lamp if her back peels and nobody's nails are close enough to scratch and pick the dead skin away. Nobody's fingers to roll the dry leaves off her shoulders. Her freckles deserve a count before they all disappear. She craves a soak in the bath. Aniseed and cucumber. The breeze smells fresh.

The heart of the sunflower on her hotel balcony bends for a last glimpse of sun. She knows sunflowers grow stronger in the wind. Tough roots. Thin soil. The flower-box flowers of lavender and sunshine yellow raise petals for her to sniff. The phone doesn't ring. Her ear falls asleep on her palm.

She sweats just enough to stick to those confidential papers. Dental records. Transcripts. Insurance-company doctors asking their callous questions. She knows Abby checks the mailbox for her insurance claim, then back into the kitchen to swallow her pills. Brittle. The nerves of Abby's finger deteriorate every day. The convulsions swing up to her arm.

§

The Sweet Tang of Success.

Three days after her accomplishments at the Unionized Safeway Workers meeting, Banana Tray Hair has confidence enough to decide to ask Room Service Boy out for a night of bowling. Bowling relaxes her, and the swirly five-pin ball fits perfectly in her hand. Cool to the touch.

She imagines Room Service Boy – with his purple dickie bow tie, room service jacket and crooked cuffs – to be quite adept in the ways of five-pin bowling. She can tell this by the way he handles a tin of soup. A strong and secure grip, but not too strong – a bowling ball won't give extra spin with an aggressive squeeze. A gutter ball or a banana split comes with an over-anxious grip. A two-four split. Very tricky. His hands exhibit a gentle certainty, perfect for the game of five-pin bowling – a prime candidate for the Youth Bowling Association.

Banana Tray Hair has seven trophies from the Youth Bowling Association. Some of the more notable ones include VOLUNTEER and FOURTH. She dusts them regularly, especially the largest of the seven on the window ledge beside her sagging single bed. It reads 2ND HIGHEST SCORE UNDER-SIXTEEN GIRLS CITY CHAMPIONSHIP.

Banana Tray Hair wonders if this second-place trophy is larger because of the size of its title. Receiving a well-crafted structure of faux-marble, brass and real plastic made her dance.

In the course of regular dusting, she notices a similarity between the tiny bowling figurine adorning each trophy.

All of them look oddly alike.

Banana Tray Hair realizes her trophies aren't all for the same aspects of the game. Nosing in closer to the androgynous, minute bowlers in mid-toss, she picks at some flecks of gold. Shellac flakes off the trophy she got for giving out free orange drink all day. Shellac all the way down to the floor.

The orange drink stained her hands for three days. She told the Safeway people she ate too many carrots and about how carotene absorbs into the skin. A medical issue.

'You must be able to see through walls by now,' they said.

'Yeah, right. I can see through walls by now,' she replied.

§

Ride Like the Wind.

Delano bent down to wipe a spot of Paper Boy blood from his black-and-white wingtips. Hauling that sack of potatoes up six flights of stairs had stuck the inside of his puce shirt to his chest. Silky heaves. His London Fog was drying in the corner, still damp from morning rain.

He solemnly declared, 'My office is now closed for the day. Please, Miss, if there are any calls for appointments, please inform clients that I will not be available until further notice. Nor do I have any other dental surgeon of my ilk to refer them to. Those clients will, much to my chagrin, have to wait.'

Delano disappeared from time to time.

He continued. 'Miss, you will be the second to know when I return. I, naturally, will be the first. Might I add you are absolutely ravishing in pink, so it would be best to change out of that chartreuse traffic jam you call a dress and find something pink and wholesome to wear.'

Delano bade a fond afternoon to an empty wooden chair and desk, where the telephone with no ringer sat. He had ripped the bells out of it years ago - too hard to concentrate with bells going off all the time. A dentist needs a steady hand.

Clinking the door shut, he found himself sitting at the bottom of the concrete steps in front of his building. The air smelled like lunchtime so he removed a silver flask of port from his breast pocket. The cap eased itself into his other hand as he sipped.

A piece of broken dental floss had been pinching at his back teeth all morning. He hoped the warm sugars of the deep violet fruit wine would melt the floss away. But this - along with movements of tongue, a folded matchbook and a dirty fingernail - did not work.

'Maybe the breeze will loosen my teeth a little,' he said to his flask.

The flask responded by filling his mouth again, out to the cheeks.

A real candied apple.

'I want a bike. I haven't ridden one in years.' He trawled up and down the sidewalk, waiting for a good one to go by.

Slowly, two wheels became feasible. Banana seats, rainbow streamers, granny bikes and ten-speeds. Ten-speeds! Silver ones, orange and purple ones, with front and back brakes and a freewheel to spin legs backwards, if required. From the step he spotted well-taped racing bars, some even turned upside down. Crazy hippie types were riding near storm drains with no hands! In bellbottoms! And the road rolled down to the river so smoothly.

Delano stood up, choked his crimson tie to his neck and spoke down to his feet. 'I want a bike, feet. I'm tired of you two.'

Without further notice, he fixed a solid pewter-tipped walking stick to the throat of a young man with greasy hair hanging off his head like Raggedy Andy.

'Just like fishing,' Delano said to his walking stick. The bike careened to a stop by hitting the wall of his building. The back wheel clicked and spun. The racing bars required a straightening, for certain.

Leaving the man to gag all over the sidewalk, Delano spoke to a second flock of cranes gathering that day. 'This young vagrant tried to steal my wallet in front of my very own place of business! Therefore I think it's quite acceptable I steal his bike. In fact, I deem this white CCM Supercycle to be mine. It used to be his, but now it is mine. An eye for an eye is a bike for a wallet.' Delano tapped his walking stick to sparks before tucking it under his arm. 'I'm going for a spin now, to loosen the old teeth a little. There's nothing to see here anymore, folks, keep moving along, and make way. Third Floor. Door on Left. Complete Confidentiality. Leave a message with Miss. Gone until further notice. She sure stops traffic in pink chiffon, let me tell you.'

In a wobble or two, the bike began to find its momentum. A faint circle of applause left him to spin his way down the sidewalk. His feet couldn't quite touch the pedals without stretching his groin, so Delano thought it best to coast awhile, cradling his walking stick in the fine curve of the racing bars. He liked the sound of his tie flapping in the breeze.

'I bet I loosened his teeth a little,' Delano said.

He whizzed past barking dogs the size of cats and garbage cans and sidewalk trees. Some passersby managed to spill entire bags of groceries, exploding Canada Dry and rolling shiny red Macintoshes down the street. Delano hadn't ridden a bike in years. His tie swung to and fro. His pant legs danced above tired argyle socks. The chain was good and greasy.

All those rigid shopping people distracted him, clearly in his way – a bunch of cardboard cut-outs – so he switched to asphalt smooth as ribbon. Racing tires hummed to a straight and yellow centre line. Smooth as a drill. His knuckles turned white as four lanes of lunchtime traffic roared up the hill.

Finally, Delano reduced his speed, favouring the bothersome pedestrians. He couldn't hear what all those blurry, jumpy, dancing people were trying to say to him, celebrating his speedy arrival.

His suit jacket started to resemble a cape, his tie a crimson sail. 'Don't you worry, everyone, just make plenty of way, plenty of way. Can't you tell I'm going for a bike ride? Make way, make way! I'm on the first leg and almost to the corner. The other competitors are well behind me now. There's no time to shoulder-check. It's more than a race, it's a Supercycle!'

§

A Sprinkle Will Do Just Fine.

Banana Tray Hair never bumps into
Room Service Boy at the Lanes. Room Service Boy never bumps
into Banana Tray Hair after she drinks four Black Russians or
bowls more than three strikes in a row or picks up a spare if she has
to – even a two-four split. Very tricky. She punctuates her refined
bowling talents with a simple fist pump, left side, followed by a soft
exhalation: 'Mama needs a new pair of shoes.'

This desire echoing across the veneer of the lanes is often true,
but she knows no one's into bowling for the money. The well-
crafted trophies of Jim's Trophy Shop, rubber-stamped on the
base of each one, are reward enough.

The people of the Lanes all chipped in to buy her some proper
bowling shoes. With one leg significantly longer than the other,
one shoe requires an inch or two of extra wood for a comfortable,
level sole.

Her bowling shoes are her only lasting shoes.

Banana Tray Hair wore her special bowling shoes to Safeway
quite frequently, until the evening a ten-kilogram green-and-
yellow paper satchel of Robin Hood All-Purpose White Flour
mysteriously exploded in the middle of Aisle 6.

The public-address system called her over to safety-watch the
mess, at least until staff arrived with proper cleaning materials: a
nice wide broom, a dustpan, a cloth for wiping down littered shelv-
ing and product, and, of course, orange signage urging caution. In
her comfortable bowling shoes, size seven, Banana Tray Hair
turned down the aisle toward the settling cloud. Wooden soles
polished hard and flat did not combine safely with the granite floor
of Aisle 6, hard and flat and lightly sprinkled with Robin Hood All-
Purpose White Flour.

What's best for a breadboard isn't best for a back.

'I can see through walls now,' she muttered.

With the extra time off work, Banana Tray Hair had ample time to think of new kinds of shoes to wear – maybe boots, knee-high, shiny, with zips up the side. Platforms and suede. Maroon. Noticeable.

Her bowling shoes provide desirable style and comfort, but safety throbbed most beneath her damaged hair.

As her seven trophies gathered dust and shed their gold, the breeze turned to leaves. A sweep of flour. For a time, she dreamed about curling instead of five-pin.

Those curling shoes are soft.

§

Pancake Banter.

Abby returned from the Independent Grocers Association in a Checker Cab. Balanced with two large brown paper bags in each arm, she let her chin guide the way up the driveway to the front step. She refused the cabbie's offer of help.

Pushing right through to the kitchen without removing her shoes, she put the tins where the tins went in the cupboard with no doors. Quietly. Vegetables and juice of orange and apple went in the fridge. Young Young Miss Lamp would not drink frozen juice from concentrate. As a connoisseur of juices, she was able to smell the difference.

A large plastic bag of powdered milk crystals bulged under the sink. Abby put two containers of cottage cheese into the fridge. Cottage cheese and powdered milk required stirring before eating – Abby enjoyed saving money and burning calories simultaneously.

Being an aficionado of cheese, Young Young Miss Lamp was curious about its relationship to a cottage. She imagined a wooden hut where diminutive people with pointy grey beards and monocles attached to tiny vest pockets stirred bubbles of curds and whey in huge iron cauldrons all day long. She'd never been to a cottage before, so she kept her story quiet. Her mouth stayed shut even though Abby tried pushing lumpy spoonful after lumpy spoonful in there. Airplane sounds didn't work. Spoons don't have propellers. And even if they did, the whole operation seemed far too dangerous. No airplanes allowed.

She chose to stare at her cool glass of well-mixed powdered milk. It had a calming blue tinge to it, and no matter how long her mom stirred it, there were always soggy little blobs of white goo clinging to the bottom of the glass. If Abby said, 'Finish your moomoo, dear,' the end swish stuck to Young Young Miss Lamp's tongue, just like cottage cheese.

With groceries properly put away, brown paper bags folded in three and shut in the paper-bag drawer, Abby expected her daughter's question-filled arrival: 'Can I do anything to help, Mom? Can I fold the bags?'

'She's a sleepy one today. It's almost noon.' Abby raised her chest and her voice followed. 'Time to get up, dear. I'll cook you silver-dollar pancakes.'

Abby cooked pancakes for brunch every other Saturday.

Two weeks ago, Young Young Miss Lamp ate thirteen and a half pancakes at her very own TV tray. Such behaviour disgusted Grandma. Pure gluttony.

'Does she need to eat so many, for Christ's sake?'

'She eats them because she enjoys them. They're only small.' Abby knows when her daughter is hungry.

'And all that sugary, sickly sweet Aunt Jemima syrup. The least you could do is buy some real goddamn maple syrup.' The colour of real maple syrup reminded Grandma of malt vinegar.

Abby slid two more silver-dollar-sized pancakes onto a busy-looking plate with a flip of a spatula. The small cast-iron frying pan bled warmth into her tea towel and she remembered to breathe. 'At least she eats. And if you want her to have real maple syrup so bad, well, you go ahead and pay for it, you bi-, bit-'

'Thanks, Mom, number thirteen and number fourteen. I think I'm going to break the record.' Young Young Miss Lamp dove in with her fork.

'Spit it out. Come on, show some spine.' Grandma dove into a half-pint of vinegar as she rocked to and fro in her spindly, creaky chair with its upholstery of dirty lemons, limes and pineapples. The silver-dollar-pancake-eating champion did not spit out number thirteen. She ate the freshest one first, an apparent secret to her success. Young Young Miss Lamp refused to spit it out.

Abby squeezed that frying pan in her left hand. Aching tendons choked 'bitch' back down her dry throat. Her finger began to shake. Had she dropped the pan, it would have burnt the floor.

'Come on, Abby, spit it out. Can you say it in front of your piggy of a daughter? Hmmm?' Rolling her eyes enough to expose the bloodshot, Grandma pinned her stare to Abby's apron. 'Same as your father too. No guts. Say it! You can't walk away for long. Go on, say it. No guts, Abby Lamp. Jesus. Your daughter's got more backbone than you do! Don't you, girl? Set an example for the child, Abby dearest. How's she supposed to grow up tough and strong with you bawling around the house all day? Eh? Tell me, I'm all ears.'

Abby bit her lip, refusing to spit it out.

'Wait. I'll tell you, save you all the heartache. Bitch. Bitch. Bitch. That's it, isn't it? An old and nasty bitch. Say it, Abby, it would do you some good.' Grandma's ears were very red.

Young Young Miss Lamp didn't finish silver-dollar pancake number fourteen.

§

To Be a Mountie.

Miss Lamp turns another page of the second transcript of her mother and Dr. Steeves.

'And you're sure it was the needle?'

'I am sure. You know this, doctor.'

'As for this numbness, which you experience in your left arm, there's no history of early stokes for the women in your family, is there? For the record, please clarify.'

'No.'

'Besides the occasional sleeping pill, and that is occasional to be certain, did you use any other drugs or medications in the weeks prior to receiving this needle?'

'No. I was in Grade 5.'

Dr. Steeves checks his list. 'Excessive drinking?'

'I was in Grade 5.'

Dr. Steeves checks his list twice. 'Oh. Pardon me. I meant currently ... any – '

'I don't drink.'

'Exposure to noxious substances?'

'No.' Abby's finger started to burn.

'Did your mother use thalidomide during her pregnancy with you?'

'I was born before they used it.'

'Is there history of psychological conditions in your family? Depression, nervous breakdowns?'

'No more than the next.' She tapped at the brown veneer in the small white room.

'Physical trauma? A car accident perhaps?'

'Not yet.'

'Physical and/or mental disability?'

'Only my finger.' Abby placed her right palm on top of her left fingers, thinking about giving Dr. Steeves the middle one.

'How are your sleeping patterns, Abby?'

'How are yours?'

Miss Lamp imagines a needle of freezing solution squelching behind the gum of her mother's molar number three, left side. She gives her blue toenails a wiggle and curls them under her feet – toes in. Special shoes gave her sore ankles and bags under her small brown eyes. Impossible shoes to sleep in.

So Miss Lamp sleeps on her stomach, and her feet are free to roll around the clock, not stuck at ten and two. Her feet rest on either side of twelve o'clock perfectly well.

'Botticelli weeps for my hips,' she says, as she rubs her flannel Mountie pyjamas.

§

A Good Girl Scout.

Young Miss Lamp spat on her fingers and rubbed at the stain on her dress. Straightening out the sunshine-yellow hem to her knees, she stood in red shoes on the curb. The bakery on the corner of the hill invited a long blink. Next to her feet, two perfect oranges rolled to a stop. She opened her purse and placed them side by each. Stealthily. An unlucky grapefruit split its sides pink.

Up the street, bread from the bakery lay strewn about the sidewalk. A man of at least sixty picked up two baguettes only to stab them back into a ripped paper bag. A girl knelt down to tap the hand of an old lady knocked flat on her back. Crusty rolls crunched beside the wheels of a baby carriage while a ceramic plant jar unable to hold its daisies got pushed back together with a straw broom. Streams of wine trickled away from the shards and powder of green glass, and Young Miss Lamp's temples throbbed to the smell. Sour grapes. A skinny man crouched below a rust-brown Ford Pinto to pick up several bruised apples.

A broken maple branch spread its leaves on the warm asphalt to rest. Before sticking the branch in the garbage, Young Miss Lamp stood the garbage can upright.

'Oh. Thank you. I was about to do it myself, but I don't think my old back could handle the strain.' Flower Shop Lady was re-potting tulips as Young Miss Lamp approached. Young Miss Lamp felt a strong hand upon her shoulder. 'Thank you so much.'

'That's okay, it wasn't too heavy. The wind must have knocked it over.'

Flower Shop Lady grew a little taller. 'The wind? Let me tell you, the wind hasn't done that since last summer, all that hail bouncing down everywhere – some of it was the size of eggs. I almost lost my window. Wind? Not today, young lady. This was stronger and stranger than the wind could ever be.' Flower Shop Lady was not going to stop. 'This was a man on a Supercycle. He had a lance!'

Young Miss Lamp tiptoed closer to the tulips opening in the early afternoon sunshine. The red ones were accentuated by the caking of rosé on Flower Shop Lady's lips. Those two lips continued, 'I mean it was a tornado. This short fellow on a big two-wheel bicycle. He couldn't even touch the pedals, with his fat red tie all flapping in the breeze. He said he was in a race with a Supercycle. After he blasted through, we all stood like fawns, gawking at each other – too afraid to move – waiting for the next racer to come through. He said there'd be another one. There's always another one in a race like that.'

§

Aromatherapy.

Paper Boy with the gold tooth that the ladies like opened his lunchtime bag and said, 'I wish I could eat something now.' His mouth watered at the sight of that dill pickle. The snap and crunch of it, the sideways twist of the tongue, the way it itched the roof of the mouth, all the while keeping suspiciously dry. Saliva dripped onto the lapel of his standard-issue navy dress coat. The freezing hadn't worn off yet. He tried a bite of his lip for feeling. Almost. Certain he would eat at some point today, a ten-count of hyperventilation – with lunchtime bag placed firmly over nose and mouth, a mélange of mustard, rye, apple skin, Montreal smoked meat and dill – tided him over. Busy Man probably missed his lunch.

The march of suits and crinkling of lunchtime bags and umbrella tip-taps turned to jeans, sneakers and a Raggedy Andy trying to crawl up the sidewalk with one hand, barely holding on to his neck with the other. This broken fellow used a terrible amount of time to move such a short way. Paper Boy counted ten steamboats and the greasy man moved three sidewalk squares. It may have had something to do with the words 'thief,' 'robbery' and 'police' he kept coughing out over and over. Paper Boy stood flabbergasted, listening closely:

'My mom bought it for me. Thief!'

Paper Boy hadn't heard from his mother in years.

'It was a CCM Supercycle. Robbery!'

Paper Boy had seen a nice picture of a CCM Supercycle in an old Canadian Tire catalogue under the bridge by the river.

'I've never stolen anything in my life. Police!'

Paper Boy did steal some Canadian Tire money once, at the age of seven. Ninety-three cents' worth. He couldn't buy a Big Turk and dill-pickle chips with it, so the cashier at the variety store took the funny money off his hands and gave him a gobstopper instead. Now Paper Boy stood sad enough to keep his five dollars and sniff his lunch to himself.

§

Window Dressing.

In her yellow party dress, Young Miss Lamp held a bouquet of robust orchids with petals of spotted yellow, orange and lavender.

People beamed at her as she held her bouquet. 'She must have done something nice,' they commented to one another as she strutted on by. Shopkeepers pretended to be staring out their windows, synchronizing their watches to the hands of the clock-tower clock as big as a barn. Men, especially men, had a spontaneous urge to tie their shoes. Not just one shoelace but both of them, double-knotted, nice and tight. Young Miss Lamp's red suede shoes had no laces.

§

Go Fish.

Ever since Abby had cut off the feet of her purple pyjama pants for a comfortable sleep in the Denis Brown Splints, Miss Lamp's delicate toes have remained outside the covers.

Hotel folding infuriates Miss Lamp. Sheets are tucked in and under too aggressively – much too difficult to push into. Too much of the sheet wasted underneath the bed. Her lip curls up when she is right. She sleeps best when she is correct.

Her feet used to sweat in those awful patent-leather shoes. Wet leather in the morning. Bare skin. Little toes. The monotonous tying and untying of such thin laces through tiny eyeholes was supposed to improve a young girl's dexterity. In the morning, knotted sheets around the bar of the sad shoes wrought tears and giggles and, on occasion, her annoyed little hams would pull sheets and blankets to the floor in one big heap.

Eventually, Young Young Miss Lamp tied and untied the laces herself, careful not to create knots. She learned to walk in those rigid patent-leather shoes. Strong as a screw. Those shoes scratched the pine-board floor right through the carpet. Arms outstretched, twisting to the bedpost for balance, walking. Turning to the side table, where she kept her book *One Fish, Two Fish, Red Fish, Blue Fish*. Hopping proved the most gratifying method of movement. The shiny brass bar held four screws in the sole of each shoe. Definitely not built for sleeping in either. She'd rather sit on her knees and walk like a pigeon, or a fish.

Miss Lamp reels in sleep.

§

It Takes a Licking and Keeps on Ticking.

Paper Boy practiced his line.

'Where can I find sixty-five dollars? No. "Where can I find" isn't right at all. It has to be more like "Do you know where I can find?"' He cleared his throat as politely as possible. He rehearsed with his fists clenched at his sides. A real navy boy.

'"Can I have sixty-five dollars, please, sir?" "Can I please have sixty-five dollars, please, sir?" No. Too abrasive, much too abrasive. I'll simply hold my hand out. No fists. I don't want people to think I'll hit them – what if it's an old lady?'

As the sun folded Paper Boy's eyes a little, he turned his palms out to dry. His blue coat hung nicely against the brick wall. The brass buttons were easy to spot. Making a cup of his hands, he kept his eyes closed and spoke well above his usual whisper.

'Can anyone help me out with some money? I need to get sixty-five dollars together to pay for some emergency dental work, and although food is a really nice gesture, I can't eat it right now because my teeth hurt too much. I'd prefer to get all the money, if I could, so I don't have to go back to the dentist's more than once. Thank you for your time and understanding while considering my conundrum.'

Paper Boy unfolded his eyes to the sound of singular, spacious applause, thinking it was for his timely use of the word 'conundrum.'

'That was fantastic, buddy.' A stranger tipped his hat from the crown of his head, twisting at his thin moustache. He smelled of rum-flavoured pipe tobacco. 'Yeah. I hate the dentist too. Gold-diggers. All of 'em. Keep it real, chief.'

To his collection of one thin blue five, Paper Boy added one slightly orange two, in the shape of a ball.

Young Miss Lamp had been collecting flowers. She stood in line right behind the man with the pencil-thin moustache, the man who tipped his hat.

Young Miss Lamp's lips formed the shape of the letter O. She couldn't muster a wink. She inspected Paper Boy up and down – from black matted hair to boots – ensuring nothing was broken. Seeing her again tied his stomach into knots. His grin formed the shape of a prostrate letter I.

'You have a stain on your dress,' he said. Paper Boy continued with his editorial about the state of her dress. 'You can't really notice it too much, though.'

Young Miss Lamp hadn't expected to receive a compliment from him. 'Thanks. Um, you left the hotel. Are you injured? What are you doing here like this?'

'Like what?'

'All right. I have twenty-seven dollars – use it. I can get more for you. Let me go home and come back. If you're hungry I can get you some lunch.'

'I can't eat lunch yet.'

'Here. Open your hands.'

His collection grew by one green twenty, another five and one more two. Now with only thirty-four dollars to go, his shoulders straightened up a little. A compelling jacket. Worthy of a wink. Young Miss Lamp had heard how cuts on a face add character. His uniform called for direct orders.

'Here. Hold these.'

Paper Boy held the flowers.

'I must have some change in here somewhere.' Bent to one knee, she rummaged through her well-contained red purse. 'Why is there lipstick all over everything?'

She dumped the contents of her purse beside Paper Boy's shiny boots. Paper Boy held his entire face against the light purple, dotted yellow and cinnamon petals. Light poured through the waxy paper. Pulling the bouquet away, his air filled with the smell of peach. His throat closed in a hiccup. The smell reminded him of lipstick.

Young Miss Lamp found two dimes and three pennies. She also found her silver glasses case, four crumpled tissues, a copy of *Us* magazine, lipstick, nail scissors, three packs of matches, two tampons, a broken cigarette, an empty container of minty Butler dental floss, several Q-tips, her blue book with phone numbers and addresses in it, a torpedo-sized can of Super Hold, half a pack of Wrigley's Spearmint, a city map with a strange smiley face on it, two adopted oranges, a travelling toothbrush, a green wallet, a wet T-shirt and a watch.

'Where did this watch come from?' She weighed it with her dainty fingers.

Paper Boy suppressed another hiccup when he heard the word 'watch.' 'What kind of watch?' he asked cautiously.

From one knee, she raised her brown eyes to his, then back to the watch. In the shine of the two o'clock sun, underneath a glare of rounded glass, her lips read the word 'Timex.'

'Here. Maybe you could sell it.'

§

All Peaches and Cream.

Miss Lamp's three peaches sit on the desk beside her papers. The 9 a.m. sun casts flat shadows and warmth to the room. She reaches for her thin green-rimmed glasses and props up a pillow to soothe her sore neck.

'Not as good as a water pillow,' she says.

Her turquoise toenails are free of sheets. Brushstrokes show in the sunlight – uneven and gloppy in spots, and entirely worn off her pinky toe.

'How did those peaches get in here?'

She thinks of Room Service Boy's upper lip.

§

Bingo Collar.

Lipstick cracked Grandma's lips as she got ready for bingo. Years without a kiss. The plum purple she borrowed from Abby's room showed off her grey whiskers. Her lips had never been full. Vigorous and shaky circles painted them up like Bozo the Clown. Stained with rouge, her cheeks barely supported her eyes, and her fake eyelashes no longer supported glue.

Dust stuck to the ring box next to the mirror. Dusty as Grandma's hair.

Abby didn't wear rings anymore.

Grandma picked through the ring box, ornate with carved tulips in cherrywood and lined with green velvet. Green brought thoughts of birth to Grandma. Abby wasn't an easy one. Twenty hours. No sedation. The ring box was Grandma's wedding present to Abby. Now the rings inside the box bought bingo.

Her brittle nails did not disturb the box's layer of dust. The clasp unhooked with a slight pick. When Abby went to IGA, Grandma's foggy eyes glowered over rings of engagement, gold and gem. One in particular, a soft twenty-four-carat band, had a single sharp-cut diamond in its clasp. It slid easily over the knuckles of her wizened ring finger. Opaque. Grandma sang a descending melody.

'B-I-N-G-O, B-I-N-G-O, B-I-N-G-O, and Bingo was his name-o.'

With a bow to the mirror and a flourish of Kleenex, she blotted her lips four times. The bits of tissue sticking to her whiskers tickled her lips to a thin smirk.

'Abby's not worth a ring. She's not shopping for a him. Always shopping for her piggy of a daughter. Put it to use, Abby dear, put it to use. I can get twenty cards for this snappy number.'

She gave it a purple kiss.

'It doesn't fit her anyway. Her fingers are too goddamn twitchy!'

Dirty purple fingerprints marred the mirror as Grandma got ready for bingo. Her polyester slacks smelled of red-wine vinegar. Getting to the bingo hall since the rust-brown Ford Pinto disappeared meant wearing furry sealskin boots – they went well with her baby-blue slacks. She got twenty-eight cards for the pink insurance slip. It would have been thirty-five if it weren't for the holes in the floorboard. Sealskin boots heat up in the sun.

Grandma's thin yellow scarf stuck tight beneath the skin of her neck. She scuffed the ground like a turkey, stepping on every crack of the sidewalk, picking for pennies with her eyes. She sang as her head bobbed up and down. She sang a pretty melody.

'B-I-N-G-O, B-I-N-G-O, B-I-N-G-O, and Bingo was his name-o.'

From a telephone wire, the magpie watched Grandma's new diamond ring twinkle in the morning sun.

§

Give Trees a Chance.

                        'Just the Scotch Broth today then?'

'With barley.'

'Pardon me?'

'Yes. The barley is quite tasty. You have to cook it on low, otherwise it will burn.' Banana Tray Hair scans the can, spying Room Service Boy's sturdy hands and purple dickie bow tie. Five-pin in style. She polishes her name tag with her thumb. Safeway is unseasonably quiet and Scotch Broth with Barley is not a big seller. 'And burnt barley smells like popcorn and who likes popcorn soup?'

Popcorn soup. Banana Tray Hair wonders what popcorn soup tastes like. He must know how to cook, as he takes extra care to heat soup on low. She never knew a man to cook soup on low. They're always in a hurry. 'How much?' She always has to tell them at least twice. Rush. Rush. 'Do you think my wife will like these flowers, Miss?' Not if you buy them at Safeway, sir. Cheap bastards, she thinks.

'Do you need a bag, sir?'

'No. I enjoy saving trees.'

'The bags are plastic, Soup Boy.'

Upon hearing the words 'Soup Boy' slip from her lips, he memorizes her name tag, sure to get it right. Room Service Boy takes pride in his efficiency.

'Well, ma'am – I mean, Lucy – ma'am, plastic bags are detrimental to our forests, not to mention the many species of birds who call trees home. Plastic gets in their way. I've seen it.'

'Really?'

'Yes.'

'No. I don't believe you. That's $1.58, please. Soupy.'

'Yes. It's true. On the edge of Safeway's own parking lot! There's a young maple with a plastic bag caught in its high branches, too high to grasp. Believe me when I tell you, I tried to get at it but the tree is too young to climb on. Too bendy.'

'Do you enjoy doing that?' She pries a toonie from his sweaty hand.

'Doing what?' Room Service Boy pushes in the clip of his dickie bow tie.

'Climbing trees.'

'Ah.' He puffs out his cheeks, looking at her name tag. Her hair, a luminous yellow, rests gently upon her shoulders. He should explain himself. 'It can be dangerous, but I do it if I have to, ma'am.'

'Lucy. Call me Lucy. "Ma'am" makes me sound old.'

Room Service Boy obliges dutifully in his purple suit. 'Um. Lucy, ma'am ... I do it if I have to.'

'I can climb trees too. It's not so dangerous.' Banana Tray Hair is wearing her new maroon suede boots with zips up the side. She suspects they are useful for climbing.

'It can be, ma'am.'

'Old!'

'Lucy, I mean – it can be dangerous. Of course, it depends upon the climbing locale, the height and branches of the tree, and if there are any objects to collect – say, a cat, or a red balloon filled with helium and rice. Call them the variable factors. Very dangerous, ma'am. When I was six I landed headfirst on the picnic table. Fourteen feet.'

Banana Tray Hair checks the time.

'Was it the balloon?'

'No. Potato salad. I landed in the potato salad. Radishes. I hate radishes. They make my eyes water.'

Banana Tray Hair sets her watch by the big blue hands of the wall clock. She likes radishes. Good for the blood. 'No, silly, which variable factor were you trying to get at?'

'When I was six?'

'Yes, when you were six.' She lifts her eyebrows twice, rather quickly, while Room Service Boy twists the curls atop his egg-shaped head for an answer.

'The cat,' he replies. 'I was trying to get the cat.'

§

Pica Boo.

Young Young Miss Lamp held a yellow notepad on her lap. A well-sharpened HB pencil burrowed a hole in the cushion of the porch swing. Sun-brown grass tickled the chocolate Lab's snout as he sniffed guard over the bird door.

'Lazy dog. Lazy dog. Laaazeeee dog. You won't catch the magpie being a lazy boy. You can't fit your fat head through there anyway. What are you going to do about the picky magpie? Eh, boy?' Young Young Miss Lamp rose on dirty toes, smacking the notepad to her knees.

'Get it, boy. Get it. Get the magpie. Woo woo! There it is, stupid. Eat 'im up. Get it! Come on, boy, you can do it. Get that magpie. Woo woo!'

That magpie was nowhere near the sniffling snout of the sleepy dog. It was nowhere near the growl, snap, slobber and teeth of the dog, and not even close to the yelp, bark, leap and scratch of the dog who, unaware of his own ability to rattle fence boards, rested his head back home on the crunchy grass – guarding the bird door and lapping up the occasional gnat.

Squeaking into the swing seat, Young Young Miss Lamp removed her HB pencil from the cushion. With a dab of lead on her tongue, she proceeded to fill in her ledger.

TUESDAY AFTERNOON

Me + Magpie 3   Stupid dog 0

She erased the number 2 well in advance of writing a fresh number 3.

'Three times today. I'm close to the record.'

She put some fresh teeth marks in orange pencil paint.

'I've settled it, dog. You are too dumb to catch such a clever magpie. You could use some help. Where is that tricky magpie anyway? I'd say too tricky for you, dog. Time's up, buddy.'

Young Young Miss Lamp kept score and rubbed her tired eyes pink. She squinted past clouds of gnats and the willow tree, toward the sound of river. No bobbing magpie, hopping and picking at the dry grass. That magpie did like to pick. Last time she saw him he had a bottle cap in his beak. He had been friendly enough to swoop down and squawk at the stupid dog on the way by – without dropping the bottle cap.

Young Young Miss Lamp kept close count of all the pennies in the bottom kitchen drawer. Pizza money. Pencil money. Dirty money. When she played Rummoli with Grandma and Abby, she always won more pennies than her little hands could hold. She counted them on the kitchen linoleum one by one.

'Those would keep him busy. He sure likes to pick at shiny stuff. I wonder if he eats it.' She chewed on her pencil some more, spitting out bits of paint. 'What does he eat anyway? I need a list.' Below the three-to-nothing score of a Tuesday afternoon, she started her list with another dab of lead to her tongue.

STUFF MAGPIE LIKES TO EAT

worms

sandwich bags

ants

tuna cans

french fries

cheeseburger wrappers

chicken bones

bottle caps

pennies

stupid dogs

'That's a good start,' she said.

Young Young Miss Lamp wiggled her dirty toes, scratching at the deep scar on her finger. She wondered how the magpie got the lid off the outside garbage can. If Abby asked someone to get the broom to clean up the mess, Grandma would yell, 'Get the goddamn broom yourself, lazybones.' Grandma picked at shiny stuff too – like spots on the windows and Abby's jewellery. Abby said Grandma didn't steal the jewellery, she just borrowed it to look nice. Abby searched for her shiny rings all the time. 'I must have put them somewhere,' she would say.

Young Young Miss Lamp consulted her list and flipped another yellow page over.

'Magpie sure is a boring name. He picks and steals too much to have such a dull name.' She tapped her HB pencil on the arm of the porch swing. Pick. Pick. 'No more boring Magpie. I'll name him Pica. Pica. Much better. He has a beak, after all. Time for a new list.' With a dab, she wrote, pressing as hard as she could.

STUFF PICA LIKES TO EAT

Mom's jewellery

Grandma

'Well, that's a really good start.'

Young Young Miss Lamp snapped her fingers quick as a wink. 'Pi-ca. Pi-ca. Here, Pica. Come on, boy. Hop this way. Hop hop. Pick pick. Woo woo!' The stupid dog perked his ears up to a growl, only to sniff and snort himself back to sleep.

'Almost four,' she said.

§

A Drop in the Bucket.

As the big blue hands of Safeway's clock touch 4, Banana Tray Hair pops out her cash drawer. Room Service Boy has a cat on his mind. He holds on tight to his Scotch Broth with Barley. She hands her drawer and receipt for the day over to her supervisor with a teaspoon smile.

Room Service Boy's purple suit slinks in beside her slowly. 'It was a nasty tabby named Ned. Sharp claws and pointy ears of fur.'

'I'm not much of a cat person.' Banana Tray Hair checks the zips of her boots. Room Service Boy's eyes follow along. Slowly. 'Show me this tree then.'

'We'd have to catch a bus. It's next to my parents' house, ma'am.' Room Service Boy checks his cuffs.

'Old!' She darts her eyebrows at him. 'No. Not the tree with the cat. The bendy maple tree with the birds and the plastic bag.'

Room Service Boy points toward the automatic doors. 'It could be dangerous, ma– Lucy.'

She removes her name tag in a wince of Velcro. 'See? Lucy. L-u-c-y.' The tag is hard to miss, pinched between rose fingernails, right in front of his nose. He smells lemons.

'Your fingernails are very clean, Lucy,' he notices.

'It's not easy to do being a cashier. Dirty money. I use lots of wipes.' She holds her fingers out straight for examination. 'I try to keep them short – much better to bowl with, you know?'

'Lemons smell nice,' he notices.

He follows Banana Tray Hair out the automatic doors, noting the length of her stride. She often goes bowling if she finishes early. Not so busy on a Tuesday. Two-for-one games. Two-for-one in style. She stops next to the curb beside a long row of carts. A great place to lean. In the time it takes to remove three hairpins, she asks, 'Have you ever been to the Lanes?'

'The bowling alley?'

'Yes. Of course it's the bowling alley. What else could it be with a name like that?'

Room Service Boy thinks about a go-kart track and an Olympic-size swimming pool. Not to mention a driving school, or the neighbours who pulled his head from the gigantic bowl of potato salad and drove him to the hospital. The Lanes were impressed he didn't have a concussion.

Mr. Lane said, 'This boy's got a head hard as a coconut – he'll be a fine linebacker one day. Fourteen feet down and he lands right in the bucket. Not a stitch! I'd say the salad broke his fall. Good shot.' Mr. Lane stopped short of tapping him on the head.

Mrs. Lane said, 'Where's your mother these days, young man? I haven't heard from her in weeks.'

Then Mr. Lane tapped Mrs. Lane softly on the shoulder and spoke right in her ear. 'Lois. Shh. Be quiet. You know she's been seen with the dentist who steals people's teeth.'

'Oh. I didn't know. How am I supposed to know that?' Her cheeks matched her shoes.

'Yes you did, Lois.' Mr. Lane smiled at the curly-haired boy with the ice pack wrapped to his head and gently returned to his wife's ear. 'It's been all over the paper.'

Mrs. Lane pulled away. 'Jeez. You can't believe everything you read.'

Banana Tray Hair finishes fluffing up her hair halfway across the parking lot. With three hairpins in her mouth, she says, 'So, have you been there?'

'Where?'

'The Lanes, Soupy. They've got drinks and music and glow-in-the-dark. Five-pin in style, yo.' She skips ahead a few steps. 'You should come. You're dressed awfully nice in your fine purple suit.'

Room Service Boy counts her steps. Very efficient.

'What's the matter with your foot?'

'Which one?'

'That one.' He points to her special shoe.

'My parents got a discount at the leg store. Ten percent off. Do you like my new boots? Suede. Maroon.' She pauses for show, gives him a twirl.

Room Service Boy's eyes light up like a Canada Day parade. He hears the drums in his head. French horns. Bassoons. Marching boots and maple trees.

'There's the tree! There's the tree! I told you. In the way. The birds have to fly around the plastic bag to get home. It's really not a home at all, I mean – '

Banana Tray Hair peers up at the tree. 'Maybe the bag is useful,' she says. 'It's a curtain protecting them from the breeze. I think it adds privacy.'

Room Service Boy shakes his head in disagreement. 'They're birds, Lucy. Birds crave the breeze. It keeps their feathers fresh. It might help the small ones to fly too, don't you think?' He puts his Scotch Broth with Barley on the ground with care and grips the skinny trunk of the maple.

Banana Tray Hair's living room has curtains for privacy. 'I guess so. I was simply being practical, you know, using available resources. Why would they build a nest in this tree anyway? I think it's going to fall over. It's not safe.'

Under his grip and heel, the tree swings just enough to slip from his hands. 'I can almost reach the bag.'

Banana Tray Hair is impressed. 'Should you be climbing in your nice work suit, Soupy?'

'It's okay, Lucy, ma'am. I'm done work for today.'

'Maybe I can help. I'm taller than you are.'

Room Service Boy gets to the ground in a jink, directing Banana Tray Hair to the plastic-bag side of the tree. He bends his knees, wraps his arms around her swizzle hips and lifts as high as he can lift.

§

Sign, Sign, Everywhere a Sign.

Front Desk Man soft-shoes his way to the cleaners' room in the evening, clutching his tidy square of papers. Without a knock, he stands at attention.

'The lady in Room 32 does not require her sheets tucked in. Not the blanket. Not the sheet. Not the cover. Leave them loose, and if they touch the floor, fine. Just don't tuck them in. Leave them loose. Room 32. Are you listening to me?'

Front Desk Man has one large eyebrow. Hard to miss, but Cleaning Lady does her best. He removes the thin red elastic from his tidy stack of papers and snaps it to his wrist. Holding up the top square, he waves it through the doorway.

'See this note? This note is from today. So you will have to do what it says tomorrow, unless, of course, she doesn't want cleaning service. Then you'll have to do it the next day, or whenever she requests cleaning service. She didn't say how long she's staying, so you'll have to make do. Always check for the sign on the door first. Remember the sign. That's why we have them.'

He flitters the note back in place. His eyebrow grows.

'Are you listening? The lady in Room 32. I think she's a lawyer. We don't advertise for trouble here, so fix your shirt. We can't have the cleaners walking about this fine hotel with messy shirts. So don't forget not to tuck in her sheets. Got it? Always check for the sign.'

Cleaning Lady nods. As Front Desk Man tip-taps back to his desk, she tucks her shirt bottom into her elastic waistband, straightening her collar from underneath her headphones. 'You're not the boss of me, Front Desk Man.'

§

Miss Lamp Eats a Peach.

Miss Lamp admires the three peaches on her desk. Well-rounded and bigger than Granny Smith apples. So new from the tree that one stem holds the white silk of a spider's web and two stems hold leaves. In her hands, a squeeze gives the scent of peach blossoms and fingers leave their mark. A cool pulse. Orange fleece.

Making a cradle of her flannel pyjama top, she carries them to the bathroom tap. Placing them in the sink, she turns the cold tap to a trickle. She unfolds a white cotton towel on the counter and presses it firm. Happy peaches. Water rolls in beads about their curves. Threads of silk swim reluctantly down the plughole. Stems slip out of ripe flesh. Her hands pull gently on the felt of each peach. 'Smooth velvet,' she murmurs.

She rubs and rubs until her fingers become numb. One, two, three clean peaches in a row let go of their drips. Folding the towel from corner to centre, she dabs them dry. Returning the cool scent of peach blossoms to their cradle, careful not to dent their flesh, she paces to her warm bed. One, two, three clean peaches roll into the sheets. 'Clench me in the sweetness of your reaches,' she says.

Miss Lamp trickles into the sheets, pulling the blanket up tight, gingerly shifting the peaches to the down of her extra pillow. She fingers inside her pyjama top, circling the minute, silky hairs around her nipple. 'Plashy juices,' she whispers.

Undoing two buttons of her top with cold peach fingertips, she attends to her other nipple. Hard as a thimble.

'Sweet clinches.' She reaches for a peach and opens her mouth. In a pinch of teeth, fuzzy skin pops fricative on the buds of her tongue. A dribble of nectar slips past the rise of her lips, glistening down her chin. Another bite and another fills the cup of her collarbone. She rips the flesh red, clear to pit, and pops the pit in her mouth. Sucking textures of mango from a walnut, she pulls the pit clean and places it in her belly button. She wipes her chin with a forearm. Shiny. Elbow to hand. Undoing two more buttons, she reaches to the extra pillow.

She giggles and gorges the meat of the next peach. Juice spills from her collarbone and streams down her chest, toward the warm pit in her belly button. Another bite and another and she is getting full. Holding the peach in her teeth, she sticks her hands to her ribs, then slides them down to meet the tie of those flannel Mountie pyjama bottoms.

Miss Lamp hears a dribbling, so her peach-filled head turns to the sound of the dribble. The berber outside the bathroom is getting darker. Her teeth lose the weight of a half-ravaged peach to the floor. Plop. Miss Lamp forgot to turn off the tap.

'I beseech you, peach,' she says in disdain, glancing to the floor, catching her breath. She sighs to the extra pillow, 'I suppose I should save one for later.' Thinking of Room Service Boy's upper lip, she wipes her hands on flannel Mountie pyjama bottoms.

Her deposition is before noon.

§

The Price Is Right.

Paper Boy walked to the pawn shop with his watch in one hand and his wet T-shirt in the other. His big lunch sat in his big jacket pocket. He had the pith to open the door in one pull. The pawn shop smelled like a couch cushion, and a tiny old bell went *ding a ding*. Young Miss Lamp's robust orchids and tight yellow party dress were etched in Paper Boy's mind. He didn't mind the Coca-Cola-and-Captain-Morgan stain on her belly when she bent down on one knee. Not one bit.

'Can I help you?' asked the burly Pawn Shop Man, supported by hairy knuckles. His head groaned over the glass display counter. He noted the cut of Paper Boy's jib.

Paper Boy used caution.

'What happened to your cheek, my friend?' Sensing vulnerability was Pawn Shop Man's strong suit.

Paper Boy found rows and rows of watches under the glass display case: digital, ticking, calculators.

'A watch, eh? Well, you've come to the right place.' Tuning in to consumer preference was another of Pawn Shop Man's strong suits.

'How much?' Paper Boy asked, holding in a stomach grumble, pointing to no timekeeper in particular.

'Which one?' Pawn Shop Man's pea-sized eyes found the finger hole in the panel door and slid it open.

Paper Boy paused. 'The Timex.'

'Ooh. The Timex. You have a discerning eye, young man. These babies sell hotter than hotcakes. Durable.' He removed it from under the counter, draping it stylishly over his hairy knuckles. The cinchy metal strap caught on a rogue hair. 'Goddammit.' He shook the watch to the floor.

Paper Boy's impatience grew.

In a clink and a wheeze, Pawn Shop Man returned to his hairy knuckles. 'Oh yes. The Timex.' He floated the Timex gracefully up to his wrist in a slight circular motion, conjuring the dim fluorescence of the curious shop in its face. 'You have a discerning eye. These babies sell hotter than hotcakes. Durable.' He flicked at its glass face and held it up to his ear, focusing on a trombone hung from the ceiling with fishing line. 'Yes. Timex. It takes a licking and keeps on … um.' Actualizing a product's sales slogan was not one of Pawn Shop Man's strong suits.

'How much?' Paper Boy was certainly hungry.

'This little baby here? Almost new. Durable. Very durable. Exceptional band.' Pawn Shop Man's head nodded from side to side, clicking like an abacus.

'How much?' Paper Boy tapped his foot.

'How much?' There was an echo in the shop. 'For you, my friend, forty dollars, no tax.'

'Forty dollars?' Astonishment caused Paper Boy injury.

'Yes. Forty dollars, eighty brand-new. Plus tax. Over half price off for you, my friend. No tax.'

Paper Boy opened his hand, raising it above the glass countertop. A fresh Timex appeared right under Pawn Shop Man's nose. 'How much for this one?'

'Mm.' Pawn Shop Man plucked the timepiece away. Daintily. 'Also a Timex.' He held it close to his discerning ear. A definite tick, not a sweep. 'It has a nice leather band, almost new.' He began to add. 'Where did you get it?'

'It's mine.'

Pawn Shop Man added two plus two. 'Why aren't you wearing it then?'

'My watch wrist hurts.' Paper Boy's wrists were covered in silly red doodles. Fresh forearms.

Sensing opportunity was another of Pawn Shop Man's strong suits. 'I also have some nice pocket watches. Gold, with a chain.'

Paper Boy had to pay for the gold in his mouth. 'How much for my watch?'

'Twenty dollars.'

Paper Boy frowned at twenty dollars. 'I need thirty-five dollars,' he said.

'Twenty dollars.' Pawn Shop Man held firm.

'Twenty-five?' Paper Boy pressed his tone.

'Twenty-two, because I like you.'

'Can I get thirty-five dollars please, sir?'

Pawn Shop Man rolled his ballpoint eyes and smiled. 'The watch and the jacket. I'll give you thirteen for the jacket, because I like you, my friend.'

Paper Boy picked at the brass buttons of his sharp-looking jacket, sighed, turned his back and picked the buttons open, one by one. He forgot to empty the deep pockets of that former sailor's jacket. That jacket held a big lunch and an orange plastic pill bottle full of Demerol. That jacket stopped traffic.

Silk and polyester navy blue turned into a damp T-shirt smelling of peach lipstick and Pilsner. And Pawn Shop Man's cash register went *ding a ding*.

Paper Boy did remember to cram his new thirty-five dollars on top of his old thirty-five dollars down into the pocket of his pants. On his way out, he had the pulp to open the door in one push.

§

Mining for Yukon Gold.

Miss Lamp wraps her thirsty towel to her chest. From her makeup bag she removes a sandwich bag of Q-tips. She prefers to clean her ears with cotton bound tightly on a pokey little stick. One end for each ear canal. This technique allows the Q-tip to rest in her ear while she brushes her teeth, applies skin moisturizer, plucks her eyebrows and fills her travel bag with extra towels.

Miss Lamp keeps her ears free of potatoes. Grandma told her that potatoes have no place in a young girl's ears.

Miss Lamp unfolds her slacks on the bed. The sight of a single peach on the extra pillow makes her thighs quiver. 'Later,' she says, 'I'll save it for later.' Her lemon blazer will complement the Indian-red leather of her litigation bag, proving red and yellow do go together, absolutely.

With two hours until her deposition, Miss Lamp tightens her towel to her chest and slides the Delano file beside her. 'I'll bet he used a dirty needle. Crooked bastard.' She furrows her brow, leafing through the transcripts of Dr. Steeves and Abby. 'A whack of volts, eh, Mom? I'd give them both a whack of volts.' She turns the page. 'So you've learned to simply cope with your new physical condition then, right, Mom?' Some dental-insurance companies could afford to pay for the twitch of Abby's finger, others could afford to pay for the Peachland Hotel.

Miss Lamp counts her pennies.

Then there's Delano the thief. Missing teeth. Rubies and gold. The alcoholic keeps them in a shoebox, apparently. Precious teeth in a shoebox rattle like the back seat of that rust-brown Ford Pinto. Class-action suits worry Miss Lamp.

So Miss Lamp's heart leaps to her throat when the phone rings. With her towel slipping its place, she jams the telephone receiver into the Q-tip at rest in her ear. Firmly. Right down the ear canal. Hammer and anvil. Hammer and anvil. She hits the floor in a heap.

The doctor says she perforated her eardrum.

§

Long in the Tooth.

When Miss Lamp comes to town, Delano squeaks open his garage door.

In his crimson bathrobe and padded slippers, he sets his precious tumbler of Scotch upon his shoebox full of precious teeth. He dusts off the seat of his white Supercycle with his sash. 'I'm tired of you two,' he says to his slippers.

Stretching a leg over the crossbar, he wheels to a rusty spade in the corner. He places the garden implement under his arm and turns to a slow roll down the gravel driveway, right to asphalt. With a miraculous one-handed U-turn, Delano spins back up the driveway, wheeling past patio stones. A bump beyond the backyard gate and Pica squawks over his head. The Supercycle crashes into a cherry tree.

'I forgot my box,' he coughs, brushing bits of black bark and mashed cherries from his bathrobe.

Straightening the handlebars just so, he straddles the seat once more, clicking back through the backyard gate. His bathrobe gleams in the sun. Waves of silk sail into the garage. A quaff of Scotch cools his lips.

In the shade of the floor, Delano opens his box of prized teeth. 'Hello, Mrs. Jones! How's your new filling, Uncle Bob?' He closes the box and climbs to his tired slippers. Balancing girth and box on his sturdy ten-speed, he repeats the journey into the backyard, coasting safely to rest under the canopy of the cherry tree. Its thirsty veins are pulling up the sod. The edge of the rusty spade proves useful in carving a medium-sized X on its trunk.

From the gate, Pica spies the gleam of Delano's sash.

Delano stomps twelve paces west and begins to dig. Delano digs and digs. His muddied slippers push the spade deeper. The snap and ting of thin roots pulls sweat from his pumpkin forehead. Real seedy. A pile of dark earth forms at his feet. 'No roots here,' he says, as he continues to dig. 'Night-night, Johnny McKay, and Ms. Rita Leachy. Sleep well, Uncle Frank.' He shakes the shoebox one last time and gurgles at its rattle. 'Four hundred and two, four hundred and two!' he exclaims, removing the tooth box's lid to rant in fives and tens and twenties. He scoops up numbers in his palms.

Delano clicks his mouth wide open and reaches in his silk pocket for his yellow-handled pliers. Pliers to grip his golden incisor.

Delano tugs and tugs.

Elbows squeezing ribs.

Delano tugs and tugs.

In a spit of blood, his tooth plops in with the rest. He cleans his face on his sleeve. 'It didn't fit right anyway, Mr. Harper, and don't you try to say it did. There's four hundred and three.' Delano stares into the box of shimmering gold and gems. 'On second thought, I'll keep you with me.' He retrieves his tooth, which used to be Mr. Harper's tooth, to rest in his silk pocket. 'Four hundred and two will have to do.'

Pica bops closer to the pile of dark earth.

'What the hell do you want?'

Pica doesn't say.

Delano ties his crimson sash around the shoebox in a nice tight bow. The earth is damp on all fours.

§

The Quicker Picker-Upper.

Room Service Boy walks with a certain amount of pride in his step. He helps Banana Tray Hair save birds from plastic-bag trees. The bag wasn't such a huge deal for her in the first place, but Banana Tray Hair had never been swept off her feet by a boy before. Especially a boy in a purple suit and a matching dickie bow tie. A boy who specializes in room service. Her bedroom has curtains for privacy too.

Room Service Boy's cuffs are straight and virtually stain-free. He notices her clean cashier nails and the scent of lemon-fresh Handi Wipes. He notices.

She fantasizes about holding his hand.

A perfect specimen.

'Thanks for your help, Lucy, ma'am.' Room Service Boy is much obliged. 'These birds will be way happier now.'

Banana Tray Hair forgets to mention the emptiness of the nest. During the nine steps it takes to get from the tree to the street, she asks, 'So, are you coming to the Lanes with me?'

Room Service Boy checks his cuffs. The letters L, A, N and the top part of an E are clearly visible above the arbutus tree. Room Service Boy had forgotten all about bowling, but he can see the sign.

Banana Tray Hair stands on one foot. 'You should come. It's cheap right now. Two for one. They have drink specials. Black Russians, B-52s, Kamikazes.'

Room Service Boy remembers his friend Oleg from Grade 6. Oleg was from Somalia. Oleg wasn't Russian but he had to leave his country because Communism didn't allow Oleg's father to sell tires at a fair price. Two for one. He looks Banana Tray Hair in the hair. It's covering her face. The wind picks up.

A flamingo's dream.

'Come on, it will be divine. Don't worry if you can't bowl, I'll help you.' She darts her eyebrows twice in rapid succession. 'You have nice, strong wrists anyhow. You must carry lots of trays at the hotel.' She fantasizes about grabbing his wrist and giving it a squeeze. A perfect specimen to shoot a straight arrow.

'Yes. Yes I do carry lots of trays at the hotel,' he says, as a matter of fact. 'The Cook is a marvellous cook. He's also a dancer.' Banana Tray Hair grabs that wrist and squeezes it. Room Service Boy's hands go wet. His heart taps like a kettledrum. He's leading the parade.

'Yes, you do have strong wrists.' She curls a grin behind her hair. 'I have a change of clothes in my bag ... If I'm to compete with you, I have to be as stylish as you. Especially for dancing later. I always change at the Lanes. It's a Tuesday.' She's bringing him up to her level of efficiency.

'The Cook is a fabulous dancer. I'm not sure if he can bowl, though. His nails are very clean for a cook, ma'am.'

'Old!' Banana Tray Hair manipulates Room Service Boy all the way across the street. 'Give me your arm,' she says. Room Service Boy holds out his other arm straight as an arrow. 'No, silly!' He returns his arm to his side. 'Like this.' She finally lets go of his wrist in order to bend his arm into a triangle. He isn't certain where to put his hand.

'Like this?' His elbow tickles his ribs.

'Now let my arm through,' she says.

He isn't certain of her meaning, exactly.

'Move your elbow toward me a little. There. Aaah.' She wraps her arm around his purple sleeve. Flush. Locks of golden hair rest upon his padded shoulder.

He really isn't certain what to do with his hand.

'When was the last time you were on a date?' she asks.

'This morning.' Room Service Boy considers collecting peaches for Cleaning Lady a date.

'Wow!' Certain it must be the uniform, she clutches his arm tighter still. Thick wrists. 'Do you ever date the guests at the hotel? I mean, there must be so many people to choose from.'

Room Service Boy's upper lip quivers a little. 'Sometimes.'

This morning wasn't the first time he had collected peaches for Cleaning Lady.

Under the big arbutus tree, Banana Tray Hair stops to rub its smooth skin. Her foot starts to hurt. 'Now there's a grand tree to climb. Not so many variable factors.'

'Except the traffic. One quick horn blast, and if you're not ready – well, the hospital's a twenty-minute drive away.' Room Service Boy's efficiency is on high alert.

'I guess so.' Banana Tray Hair desires another boost. He can lift her up just fine. Arms around her hips in a jiffy. Room Service Boy cools a sweaty palm on his jacket, ruminating about soup. He stops in front of the Lanes.

'Must we go bowling so soon, ma'am, um, Lucy?' He seems genuinely concerned.

'It's okay if you can't bowl,' she says. 'After a few drinks it will be easy.' Banana Tray Hair perches on one leg again and winks at him. Room Service Boy's heart rests. Like beets in a jar.

The flamingo wrings his wrist for a pulse.

'What's wrong, Soupy?'

'I forgot my Scotch Broth with Barley in the parking lot!'

Scotch Broth with Barley is not a big seller.

§

Pretty as a Peach.

Cleaning Lady's trolley of clean sheets, spray bottles, plastic-wrapped cups, pillow mints, miniature soaps and shampoos winds its way down the diamond-patterned carpet of the third-floor hallway. She sees no sign on the door of Room 32 that reads NO CLEANING SERVICE PLEASE.

Manu Chao's 'Bongo Bong' rattles in her headphones. 'King of the Bon-gos, King of the Bon-gos, hear me when I come, baby,' she sings in key, tapping her dry hands on the trolley's steel handle. She's a funky monkey. Manu's music carries her to the sharp white sands of Tavira in Portugal. Her grandfather drove a tractor full of oranges, and every day the orange trees were full. He left one, two or three oranges on the doorstep of each cottage on the island. People awaited his arrival. His orange trees were never empty.

'Obrigado!' the holiday dwellers shouted as he puttered on past the dunes. Puffs of diesel smoke framed his straw hat against aquamarine waters and the distant cliffs of Morocco. 'Obrigado para as laranjas,' they exclaimed, waving at the man who hadn't eaten an orange in all his life.

Oranges reminded him of the old war with Spain.

Cleaning Lady keeps peaches in the canvas pouch of her cleaning trolley. Room Service Boy fills her canvas pouch during peach season, and this daily act of generosity improves her singing voice. She figures her grandfather would approve of the peach distribution network. Her trolley is much quieter than her grandfather's old tractor, and guests seldom wake when she slips into their rooms before the sunshine to place a peach or three on unsuspecting tables. She works in the Peachland Hotel, after all, and although she's forbidden to bring her bongos to work, peaches and Manu Chao make her hum.

Cleaning Lady pats on the door of Room 32. Pat pat pat. Pat pat. 'Hello. Hello. Cleaning service.'

There is no response.

'Hello. Hello. May I come in?'

It's after eleven in the morning, so Cleaning Lady reels out her key ring. The door sighs open in a push. She backs the cleaning trolley into the room. A convenient door prop. Her feet squish into the carpet. 'Messy, messy, messy,' she sighs, and snaps on her rubber gloves. One. Two. She throws an old towel on the floor and places a bottle of Windex on the table. The peaches are gone. She smiles at the consumption of her fruit. She frowns at messy sheets. Near the head of the closest twin bed, her shoe sinks into the remains of a half-eaten peach. 'Pêssego feio!' she curses. It is an ugly peach.

Removing the extra pillow in a huff sends a solitary peach into the air. Cleaning Lady dives across a mélange of twisted sheets, blankets and polyester gardens. Her chin lands on the bed. Her hands form a cup. The cup holds a peach. 'Pêssego bonito!' she shouts. It is a pretty peach.

Cleaning Lady puts her rubber glove over her mouth. The peach drops and rolls gently to the side of Miss Lamp's head. Miss Lamp is nestled in between the two beds with a phone receiver in hand. 'Oh my Jesu! Lady, lady, are you okay?'

There is no response.

Yellow rubber-gloved fingers pinch Miss Lamp's rosy cheeks. Cleaning Lady can tell the woman flat on her back is breathing.

'I'm late for my guitar lesson,' Miss Lamp shouts. Miss Lamp plays guitar at a high-intermediate-advanced level on Saturdays. 'Rocky Raccoon' is her latest number.

Cleaning Lady doesn't know the words to that song. There are no bongos in 'Rocky Raccoon.' Cleaning Lady pinches Miss Lamp's cheek again.

'Ouch! Why did you do that?' Miss Lamp touches her warm cheeks, focusing her eyes on the round lips of a woman who wears curlers to work.

'You have nice cheeks.'

'Pardon me?'

'You were sleeping.'

'It's Saturday, I get to sleep in on Saturday.' Miss Lamp's eyes loll back in her head. 'What time is it?' She sticks a dry tongue to the roof of her mouth. Miss Lamp is thirsty.

'It's 11:45 in the morning.'

'Pardon me?' Miss Lamp wonders if she repeats herself.

'It's 11:45 in the morning.'

'My lesson isn't until two. My ear aches.' Tinnitus marches to the drum of that ear.

'Q-tips are dangerous. You should use toilet paper.' Cleaning Lady knows this from experience.

'What?'

'It's not Saturday either. I don't work on Saturdays. It's a Tuesday. And you should get up off the dirty carpet and put some clothes on – ' Cleaning Lady pauses to read Miss Lamp's face and towel.

Vacancy.

'Hello. Hello.' Cleaning Lady often repeats herself.

Bright yellow fingers dance before Miss Lamp's eyes.

'Can you hear me, lady?'

Miss Lamp nods in agreement.

'Do you want help up?'

Miss Lamp nods in agreement. The sensation of rubber fingers tickling her armpits brings her from her knees. A door hinge. 'I want the bathroom.' Her rosy cheeks are turning white.

Cleaning Lady sighs deeply. 'I'll clean up after you go.' Peachy keen.

'Thanks.'

Leaning into the sink, Miss Lamp removes the Q-tip from her ear. The phone on the floor rings, rings and rings.

§

Delano Gets an Escort.

Delano push-pedals his way down the street wearing his best suit of silver-grey silk. He swerves, leans and retrieves his flask. Heart palpitations come from riding with no hands, so he uses his teeth to open his flask. By a twist of his tongue, he spits the cap into his breast pocket discreetly and proceeds to swig. 'Over the teeth and around the gums, look out stomach, there it is,' he says, imbibing a warm and fruity gulp.

Delano's velocity increases with a flap of his tie.

The breeze smears syrup-spit across his chin as the wheels of his white CCM Supercycle clicks, clacks and spins – a real dynamo, carving a continuous S along the road. He sticks the stem of the flask down his throat once more, deep down to the balmy cockles of his heart. Nurturing a teat of sweet cordial, he flies right through a stop sign. A woman pushing a baby carriage shakes her fist at him in dismay. 'Why you!' she screams. 'Slow down, asshole!'

In a suckle, Delano waves hello with his shiny flask. 'It's a race!' he says, then returns to his breast pocket for the cap, screwing it down with his teeth.

The port is in his pocket.

Two hands on the bar and Delano flinches to the scream of a siren behind him – so he decides to shoulder-check. 'It is a race, and a police escort for me.' He grins profusely while the cruiser gains pavement.

Before too long, Delano favours a calculated detour. He whizzes down a footpath at breakneck speed – past jittery squirrels, screaming children and mothers far too belligerent to see a dentist regularly.

A dog runs away with its leash.

A greasy middle-aged man who has been mindful of walking

sticks for years swears he just saw his old bike fly by. Delano knows his way to the courtroom.

Crouching to the curve of racing bars, Delano grips their tape tight. 'Make way. Make way,' he says. Fresh argyle socks cling to stout calves. Pumping up and down up and down up and down. His suit starts to resemble a cape. 'I think it's a time trial. For me! Out of my way.' He begins to yell, 'Can't you tell I'm making record time?' His chain is good and greasy. He postulates upon silver pedals. 'Watch out! There's something to see here, folks!'

As the police cruiser bumps, flashes and honks its way down the footpath, past the gaping, cavity-ridden mouths of yappy mothers and their children, hidden squirrels and a greasy middle-aged man holding his throat, the humming wheels of Delano's Supercycle cuts a garter snake right in two. Delano is fast.

Right in two.

The dog and his leash are long gone.

Delano skids in front of the courthouse, blotting his sweaty pumpkin forehead with the back of his tie. A small piece of dental floss dislodges from his teeth.

It's been back there for years.

Clicking through the automatic doors, he wheels down the hallway to the shimmer of door number four. The kickstand lets out a squeak.

Delano's belly precedes him.

'You are late, Mr. Delano.' The judge straightens his wig in line with his robe. Delano takes a seat. 'Where is your lawyer, Mr. Delano?'

'I don't care for a lawyer. I'm not a criminal.' He tightens his tie taut to his Adam's apple. Grenadine red. 'I'm a dentist,' he declares. To keep his cheeks full of pride, he removes his shiny silver flask from his breast pocket.

'You can't drink in here, Mr. Delano. This is a court of law.' The judge motions toward his crafty wooden gavel.

'And I'm a thirsty dentist!' Delano slaps his knee, then sips on some ruby-red port. 'This is a time trial and I think I broke the record.' He fills his gullet again and smacks his lips into gratitude.

'Security!' calls the judge. The bailiff takes a step. Delano slinks deep down in his seat.

'All right already. It's just grapes. Lots of vitamin C, good for the gums.' The judge stares at an old mug shot. Delano twiddles his thumbs.

'The picture of you here shows you as having a gold tooth. Clearly.'

'I always smile for a photo.'

'What happened to your tooth, Mr. Delano?'

'I ripped it out this morning and – ' Delano shuts his lips.

§

A Little Dab'll Do Ya.

                      Young Miss Lamp marked up the kitchen linoleum with the soles of her red suede shoes. Abby had a tea towel wrapped around her hand.

'Where were you?'

Young Miss Lamp held her well-contained red purse below her belly. 'You were supposed to phone if – ' Abby dropped her tea towel, revealing a shaky hand. ' – if you were going to be out late. You didn't even phone. I was going to call the police. I haven't slept all night. You are so inconsiderate.'

Young Miss Lamp played safe. 'Sorry, Mom.'

'Sorry. Yes, there's a new one. What is it this time? Did the car you were in break down? Or, or you fell asleep at your girlfriend's place and forgot to set the alarm? Am I close?'

'Actually – ' Young Miss Lamp had a real excuse this time. 'These guys from school tied up this other guy with dental floss, and he's injured. He broke his tooth and he needs money to pay for the dentist.'

'The dentist. Christ. Is that why I can smell the booze from here? What do you take me for? The dentist. Don't you ever mention those two words in this house.' Abby hadn't been to the dentist in years. Her daughter had perfect teeth. 'Go get cleaned up. Are you hungry?' Abby knew when her daughter was hungry. 'How's your new dress?'

Young Miss Lamp thought about grilled cheese and Campbell's Tomato Soup even though she wasn't hungry. 'Can I borrow twenty dollars?'

'Now go get cleaned up and I'll make you some lunch.'

'But he needs it, Mom. I feel really bad for him.'

'Then I'm sure you had something to do with it.'

Young Miss Lamp threw her well-contained red purse to the floor. 'Why accuse me? I hardly know him!'

'Well, I've never known you to help strangers, dear. Now go.'

Young Miss Lamp pushed past her mother to a dishrag and grabbed the Ajax from under the sink. She ran the rag under the tap, applied a liberal sprinkling of Ajax and gave the rag a squeeze.

'"Excuse me" works too.' Abby dried dishes carefully.

'Sorry, Mom.' Young Miss Lamp sucked in her belly and scrubbed and scrubbed that Coca-Cola-and-Captain-Morgan stain. Grey paste mixed in with the yellow of her dress. The stain grew and grew, so she added more Ajax. 'Mom?'

'Would you like cream of – ' Abby dropped a teacup. It tinkled on the floor. 'Your dress! What the hell are you doing?'

'I spilled some Coke on it. Don't worry, it's coming out.'

'Stop it. Stop! You're bleaching it!' Abby snatched the dishrag away. 'You've ruined your dress. It was brand-new. Thanks a lot.'

Young Miss Lamp scowled. 'It was coming out, Mom.'

'Stupid as your grandmother.'

'Excuse me?'

Grandma's palliative care broke Abby's bank.

'Go out and drink all night. I don't care. Just go.'

'I think the dress will – '

'Just go!' Abby's arm began to convulse. Electrically so.

'Well, why don't you go cry some more then?' quipped Young Miss Lamp.

From inside Abby's purse, and inside Abby's wallet, Young Miss Lamp plucked two crisp, green twenty-dollar bills. She kicked at the shoes on the mat.

The wooden screen door smacked shut.

Lollipop, Lollipop, Oh Lolli-lollipop.

'What's this?' Delano sniffed at his tie. His liver spots matched his tie. The spots on his tie matched the blood from Paper Boy's gums. His forehead mirror was speckled and foggy like salmon skin. The mirror's black elastic dug red lines deep into his sweaty brow before his wrinkled suit pants found the plastic cracks of the big old chair.

Stretching to the limits of his argyle socks, he clacked and flapped his wingtips together like a Dorothy. Undoing the top button of his pants, he began to scratch his belly. The big old chair squeaked. Delano scratched and scratched his belly red. He strangled his tie to the base of his neck.

The liver spots on the back of his hand swam a salamander swim. The sun peered in on his open belt buckle, illuminating a dance of eczema. He counted liver spots and picked them purple. Seven.

Delano's cracked and yellow nails scraped against his belly.

An alligator-skin belt slithered out of its noose.

He poked the needle of an empty syringe past the foil cap of a small glass bottle, anticipating the taste of onions on his tongue.

Onions reminded him of lunchtime cheeseburgers. As the syringe spilled into his belly, he winced deep enough to show Mr. Harper's gold tooth. Delano held tight to his alligator-skin belt. Eventually, he sat up, with wrinkled suit pants gripping his thighs and a drip of blood seeping into his puce shirt. He adjusted his forehead mirror accordingly, tapping his wingtips to the floor, as if to stand.

'What's this?' Delano's pants slipped past his knees. Paper Boy stood at some distance, holding out his hand.

'I have the money for the tooth.' Paper Boy had been uncrinkling his seventy dollars long enough to stand within reach of

Delano's pewter-tipped walking stick. Right there in the corner next to the London Fog on a brass hook. He knew how to use it if he had to. Phantom pain for a squeaky wagon, or a ribbing.

'Seventy dollars, eh, boy? Ooh, big bones.' Delano clinched his teeth together and clacked his heels. His pants at his ankles. His puce shirt, a gown. Delano's wizened temples framed pupils fat and black. 'Close the blinds please, Miss. I can't add with all this racket.'

Paper Boy inched toward the rib-cracker. There was no Miss in the room. 'I have the seventy dollars for my gold tooth. I'll just put it on the – '

'Oh no you won't!' Delano took a step closer, slapping his alligator-skin belt to his thigh. 'Seventy dollars isn't nearly enough, my young friend. Did you ever hear of tax? Do you know what happens to people who don't pay tax? Those perpetrators!' He slapped his thigh with syllabic vigour. 'You hot young whipper-snappers have no idea what happens to people of my ilk if they don't pay their tax.' He cocked his head without a blink. 'They send 'em to jail. Jail. Jail.' His thigh matched his shirt. 'Are you aware how hard it is to get a gold tooth like yours in jail?'

Paper Boy rustled his tongue over his new gold tooth. 'I'll just give you the money then.' He motioned toward Delano's empty desk and phone with no ringer inside it. Delano's head hung still with his last word.

'Jail. Oh no you won't, I say! You won't have me, I say.' Delano threw out his arm in a salute. 'Stand back, boy!' Paper Boy stood back. 'I want tax. Seventy dollars plus tax. Got it?' Delano stood at attention. A rumpled soldier with pupils as big as nickels.

Paper Boy knew a rib-cracker when he saw one. 'But you said no tax.' Paper Boy was right. 'And your sign says – '

'No tax? There's no such thing as no tax. Facts is facts, boy.' Delano slapped his belt on the wooden floor and Paper Boy left his feet. 'You know what happens? Teeth aren't easy to get. Time and labour. Time and labour and tax.' Delano checked his balance with the big old chair. 'Where'd your sharp-lookin' navy-blue jacket get to, my young friend?'

Paper Boy found his feet. 'I sold it.'

'How could you?' Delano pulled the belt tight between his meaty drumsticks.

'I sold the jacket to pay for the tooth.'

'You think sailors' jackets grow on trees, boy? I went to sea for that one.' Globs of Delano's spittle fell to the floor. Salmon spawn. 'Where's my tax? Seventy dollars, plus tax. No Refunds. Low Rates. Satisfaction Guaranteed. Have a Winning Smile.' Delano draped the belt around his neck, parted his lips and clenched his teeth again. 'Now, there's a winning smile.' He twisted the forehead mirror off his head and held it close in front his face. The back of his tie found his teeth and he polished them dry.

His lips were stuck open. An envelope of dirty Chiclets.

'Much better. Get over here, young fella, and let's have a gander at your teeth.' Delano sat in the big old chair, his pants hanging off his feet. 'Hop right up. Come on now, don't be shy. I'm your dentist.' He slapped his hand on the back of the big old chair. 'Chop, chop. I don't have all day.' Delano stuck out his neck, skin over collar. 'When was the last time you had a checkup there, fella? I'll give you a championship smile. Up you get. Chop, chop.'

'I was here this morning and would like to pay for my tooth now, if I could.'

Delano wanted his gold tooth back. 'A nice, pretty Paper Boy like you in the big house. I bet you'd sing like a raven.' Delano pushed below his belly. Paper Boy thought about cracking his ribs.

'Tax. Where's my tax?' Delano crowed.

'I have seventy dollars.'

Delano rubbed his crotch. 'I forgot to give you a lollipop.'

Paper Boy threw three thin blue fives, two purple tens, a green twenty and several orange twos to the floor. He kept the change for himself as he ran down the steps from the third floor, door on left.

§

Flower Child.

Paper Boy caught up to his windpipe steps past the bakery. The image of Delano rubbing his crotch buckled him over at the waist for a wretch. Empty stomach. Empty sidewalk, swept clean of broken glass, dirt from potted begonias, broken fruit and bread crumbs. Paper Boy didn't care for lollipops.

Pollen ruffled Paper Boy's nose. A multitude of hydrangeas, ferns and pink gerberas filled a table in front of the flower shop. He pressed his face to the large glass window, knowing nothing about flowers except how the flowers Young Miss Lamp ordered him to hold gave his a heart a lift. He forgot all about his lunchtime bag with the Montreal smoked meat on rye with mustard, pickle and the apple Busy Man couldn't eat because Busy Man's wife forgot about Busy Man's soft gold tooth every day.

'Can I help you?'

Paper Boy smudged up the window.

Flower Shop Lady tapped him on the shoulder. 'Can I help you?'

'No. I'm just browsing, thanks.' His head was fixed.

'Anything in particular? Our roses came in yesterday.'

'No. Not roses.' Paper Boy knew all about roses. The flowers Young Miss Lamp had given him to hold had no thorns, and they didn't smell of peach lipstick either.

'Would you prefer daisies? Daisies are wonderful this time of year.' She grimaced at the back of his head, noticing it needed a good scrubbing.

'No. Not daisies.' Daises are those white-with-a-yellow-dot-in-the-middle flowers. The she-loves-me-she-loves-me-not flowers.

His heart sank for daisies.

'They have strong roots, perfect for a family.' Flower Shop Lady was getting ahead of herself.

'No. Not daisies.'

Flower Shop Lady grinned her rosé-caked lips thin and sucked up a sizable gulp of air. 'Tulips. I'll bet you're after some tulips. They're not just for Easter anymore. I have single-coloured or two-tone, and they arrived only yesterday. The purple ones are so lush. What's your favourite colour?' She put her hands on her hips. 'Blue. I knew it.'

Paper Boy's eyes searched beyond the foggy glass, the entirety of his face pressed for time.

Flower Shop Lady continued with ease. 'Blue is so hard to come by. A real rarity.'

'No. Not tulips.' Tulips reminded him of the Easter Bunny. Young Miss Lamp was not the Easter Bunny. On his after-school delivery route Paper Boy once saw a tortoiseshell cat eat whole tulips right up out of the ground. He wanted flowers. Not cat food.

Flower Shop Lady had another idea entirely.

'Why don't you come inside and we can find you some nice flowers for your mother?' She tapped him on the shoulder again.

'They're not for my mother.' His cheeks flushed to red in front of the glass. The steam turned to drips. Having Young Miss Lamp bend to one knee on the sidewalk, in her yellow party dress, searching for money to give him, encouraged him to forget all about his Timex. It would hurt his wrist anyway.

He would hold flowers for her, even without orders to do so.

'Ah. I see.' Flower Shop Lady opened the door to her shop and beckoned him inside. 'We'll find you the perfect flowers for your nice young lady.'

This idea of possession frightened Paper Boy. Everything he owned he had to sell. Everything he sold would be sold again.

'Do come in. I'm certain I have the perfect flowers for her.'

Paper Boy's face stayed put.

'I'll show you through the window then, shall I?'

Paper Boy nodded into the window, bonking his head once or twice.

Flower Shop Lady was a princess of the soft sell. She presented him with roses of red, yellow, pink and white, daisies that weren't like daisies, a sunflower and tulips of orange and purple. She held the purple ones up to the window for a long time. He smudged his breath from the glass once more, in time for more puffy hydrangeas the colour of cantaloupe, gerberas of the rainbow, lilacs, lilies of the valley, carnations pink and blue, and, lo, there were the flowers that rushed his heart past his chin and right out the top of his head. She held the flowers against her smock. He scurried to the door in haste, nearly knocking a potted begonia off its perch. Ready for a hug.

'Come in. Do come in!' Flower Shop Lady exclaimed. She prepared to smile for him. 'I just knew we'd find the right ones. I knew it.' Though she wasn't prepared for the gash on Paper Boy's cheek. 'Oh my. Oh no. Oh my.' She had always wanted to be a grandmother.

'No!' Paper Boy couldn't reach the flowers in time. Cinnamon petals and lavender stamens crashed to the floor. Leopard spots on the lemon-lime orchids bent to a stop underneath her shoe.

'What happened to your face?'

'Oh, it's nothing.' He pointed to the floor. 'And the flowers?'

'It's not nothing! Oh my.' She wrung her hands together. 'We have to get your face cleaned up right away, otherwise you'll risk infection. I've got some iodine and band-aids in my first-aid kit. I'm always cutting my fingers around here. Don't you move a stitch.'

Flower Shop Lady flew away, right past her broom.

Paper Boy knelt down beside the broken petals. Picking up the flowers gingerly, with both hands, he held them to his face and sniffed in deeply. So full of cherries and nectarines that water pushed out of his eyes.

§

Pennies from Heaven.

Grandma bobbed for pennies on her stroll to the bingo hall. Pica sat on the telephone wire. The sun shone on a dime, right between her furry sealskin boots. 'Well, isn't that the bee's knees! Stupid people throwing their money away. One thin dime, they say. One thin dime is mine, I say.' Grandma got down on her hands and knees, her polyester knees scratching the concrete.

Unseasonably warm.

Prying one thin dime off its side, she slipped it into her pocket, then crawled to the edge of grass. 'Where there's a dime there's a quarter, and where there's a quarter there's another.' Grandma found a nickel underneath a patch of crabgrass. 'Oooh-whee. Now there's somethin'.' She put the nickel in her pocket and opened her mouth in awe. Two quarters side by side under a fluffy dandelion. She snapped it off at the root, wiping milky fingers on her slacks. 'Clear out, you old dandy! There's fifty cents between you and me. It's a bonanza.' She grinned and clinked the shiny quarters into her hand. 'Ooh – American.' And into her pocket they went.

Grandma patted her wrinkled hand flat to the temperate grass. Down, down, down. Pica caught a glint of her yellow silk scarf and the shiny diamond ring on her finger.

Six pennies, two more dimes, another nickel, and Pica's beak snapped onto Grandma's sparkly diamond ring. Such a shiny ring. Talons dug into her hands, popping veins and bruising tendons. He scratched and picked at the glimmering gem. Grandma tried to lift her hand and Pica pecked her in the eye.

Ten times fast.

Hard enough for her to swell it shut.

'Aaaah! Aaaah!' Grandma screamed. Pica clicked in her ear. She swung her right fist at the bird, catching a tail feather. Pica could've sheared her finger off at the knuckle and eaten that too. Polished the nail right off. He held tight to the gem as Grandma pulled hard at her hand, then at her wrist, then at her forearm. Pica stripped the bloody ring off Grandma's bloody finger.

Pica's talons squeezed in close, then let go of her hand.

A wave goodbye.

Sitting on the telephone wire with a gold and diamond ring in his beak, Pica squawked down at Grandma. Grandma's yellow silk scarf covered her eyes while she cried.

She had forgotten to wear her adult-incontinence briefs.

§

'Cause Band-Aid's Stuck on You.

Paper Boy blotted pollen from his eyes with inky thumbs.

Flower Shop Lady returned with cotton and iodine.

'Don't move a stitch, I said. Come over here and have a seat, right away. You're risking infection.'

Paper Boy held the flowers to his chest and did as told. He rested in a rickety old chair. 'What about these flowers?'

'Oh, don't worry about them.' She snatched the crooked orchids and threw them in the garbage can. 'I've got plenty more. They came in yesterday too. All the way from Thailand ... ' Paper Boy sniffed for those orchids in particular. It didn't matter where they came from. It mattered who they were going to.

She met his sullen eyes and looked down to his cheek, brushing flecks of pollen off his face. 'This might sting. Your cut calls for stitches, young man.' She tipped the iodine onto a cotton ball. 'You can hold my hand if you prefer.'

As she dabbed and wiped the stains from his face, the smell of iodine corked his throat. 'We're going to have to cover it up.' Releasing his hand, she applied three band-aids without touching the pulp of his cheek.

'Thank you.'

'You're welcome. Much better now. You can never be too careful.' She pursed her rosé lips at him. He pushed at his band-aids. 'Now. How about some orchids?'

'Yes, please.' He bolted up straight as a ruler, measuring for the garbage can.

'Not those old things, dear. We'll find you some fresh ones.' Flower Shop Lady had a good eye.

Paper Boy saw blossoms of mauve, green apple and honeysuckle. Up close, the new fresh orchids smelled of sticky tangerines.

'Can I have the ones over there too?'

'Where?' Flower Shop Lady couldn't tell where he pointed. Her other eye wasn't so good.

'In the garbage can.'

'Oh. Come now. She'll enjoy these much more.' Flower Shop Lady placed them on her counter and wrapped them in a bow of green velvet. 'Remember to give them a fresh cut, and change the water every few days. Some orchids last a month.' With the bow tied softly, she said, 'That's $4.12, please.'

Paper Boy dug deep into his pocket, spilling a plethora of change onto her counter. 'Is three dollars okay?'

Flower Shop Lady counted $2.08. 'More than enough. I gave a bunch of these to a beautiful young girl today.'

'Thank you.' He shoved the robust orchids to his face, funnelling their joy. A big Dixie cup. In a sniff, his heart lifted a little.

'She was wearing the cutest yellow dress I have ever laid my eyes on. And quite helpful.'

Paper Boy left the shop with flowers in his face. Flower Shop Lady bent at the knees and reached into her garbage can for the broken orchids.

§

Back from the IGA.

Abby wondered why her daughter wasn't sliding her bum down the stairs by now, ready to fold brown paper grocery bags and gobble up pancakes. 'Wake up, sleepyhead,' Abby said, opening her daughter's bedroom door. Young Young Miss Lamp sat on the bedroom floor in her purple-striped pyjamas. Her Denis Brown Splints tied even tighter.

'Why is Grandma mad at me?' Her tired brown eyes were worried pink. Abby knelt down beside her.

'She's not mad at you.'

'She hates my shoes.'

'Well, I don't hate your shoes. They're going to make you walk straight. You want to walk straight, don't you?'

'I guess so.' Young Young Miss Lamp sniffed and wiggled on her bum.

'Let's get these nice shoes off and I'll make you some pancakes.'

'Silver dollars?'

'As many as you can eat. Do you think you can go for the record of twelve today?'

'Fourteen. At least fourteen.'

'Fourteen! I don't know about that. Are you sure?' Abby picked the tight little knots out of the laces. Young Young Miss Lamp's ankles were aching.

'You've been playing with the laces again. Time for another shoe-tying lesson.'

'The new record is fourteen, Mom, but I'm not so hungry.' Abby loosened the laces that keep the tongues quiet. Young Young Miss Lamp slid her clammy toes out of those Denis Brown Splints. 'There's one.' Abby sniffed wet leather. Her daughter's toes always stained brown. 'And the other.' Abby tickled each tiny brown toe. 'No laughing allowed.' Abby tickled and tickled and Young Young Miss Lamp wiggled about, working on a grin.

'Don't, Mom.'

'Oh, come on. You can't keep those happy feet in there all day. I'm the tickle monster!' Abby went for the soles.

'Mom, stop. It pains.'

Abby stopped. 'Your feet will probably hurt a little. Remember what the physiotherapist said.'

'The leg doctor?'

'Yes. He said your feet might hurt in the morning.'

'My back hurts too.' The purple-striped pyjama top clung to her back. Warm, red and itchy.

'Are you sure?'

'Yes, Mom. It really pains.' Young Young Miss Lamp turned down her chin and cried. Her shoulders bounced to her exhalations. Abby didn't remember the physiotherapist mentioning anything about back pain with the Denis Brown Splints. She would have to give him a call.

'Stand up and I'll rub it for you.'

Young Young Miss Lamp tried to get up on her feet. She pushed with her hands and bent her knees stiff. 'I can't.'

'Yes you can. Come on. Don't be lazy.'

'I can't.'

'Let's go have some pancakes. I'll help you up.' Abby rose to her feet. 'Hold out your hands and push with your legs when I lift.' Young Young Miss Lamp held out her hands. 'One. Two. Three.' Young Young Miss Lamp pushed hard on her little hams. 'And up you get. Easy as pie.'

'Ow.' The sound strained on her face. 'Hug?'

'I'll rub it better.' Abby touched her daughter's back, hot and wet. Young Young Miss Lamp shook in her mother's arms. Soft as pancake batter.

'Grandma hates me,' she said.

Abby's finger rolled out in a tremor.

§

Manners To Spare.

Banana Tray Hair dissuades Room Service Boy from pining over his Scotch Broth with Barley. All with a kiss. She plants it right on his cheek. His heart beats bigger than a timpani drum. Huge, round and deep. He's the parade master.

'Shall we go inside?'

'Yes please, ma'am.'

'Old!'

'Yes please, Lucy, ma'am.'

'Much better. By the way, this door isn't automatic.'

Room Service Boy stops in his tracks.

'Ah.' He stays perfectly still, in anticipation of the door. Banana Tray Hair squeezes his arm. He gives her hand a gentle push.

'Don't be nervous, you'll do fine. I'll help you.'

'Ah.'

'Are you worried about your soup? I can get you a whole box. Safeway employee discount. I fought for it at our last union meeting.' She brushes at his collar. 'One of mine, I think.' A strand of curly blond hair takes to the breeze.

Fit for a nest.

'Are you in a union? You know what they say – work union, live better.'

Room Service Boy isn't aware of any such union for Room Service Boys. 'No.' He is hoping for the door to open on its own. Just like Safeway.

'You should be. There must be one for hotel workers. I'll check it out for you.' Room Service Boy sways to her efficiency. 'Come on. Let's go in. We're wasting valuable bowling time.'

'Thanks, Lucy, ma'– '

'Much better.'

Room Service Boy nearly rips the door off its hinges. This impresses Banana Tray Hair. 'Wow. You do have strong wrists.' The door's recoil bonks him in the head.

'Are you okay?' She's mildly concerned about the dent in his forehead.

He doesn't miss a beat.

'Absolutely, ma'am. I've got a head hard as a coconut.' Filling his chest with pride, he pulls her arm close to his purple lapel. 'I don't care for these old-school doors. I'm an automatic man.'

'Me too.' Banana Tray Hair plants a kiss on his chin, seeding a forest of drumsticks for the parade impresario. 'Automatic is the best.'

'Indeed it is, m'Lucy. Indeed it is.'

Banana Tray Hair gives him a love tap. He won't baby the ball.

§

Magpie Surprise.

Abby stepped past the wooden screen door with some chicken bones in one hand and a broom in the other. Past the wisps of the willow tree.

The aluminum garbage can sat barren in the alley. Setting the broom against the fence, she plugged her nose, lifted the lid and plopped in all the bones. She picked up her broom and sat with her back against the fence and the lid beside the can. Alley stones rolled with a subtle flick. Abby stretched in her slippers and turned back inside the yard. A peek now and again would suffice.

The chocolate Lab sniffed at the grass in front of his hole in the fence. Abby tapped the handle of her sturdy broom to the grass and counted to ten.

The stench of the garbage can seeped through the fence. Sour milk, banana peels, rancid fat and tuna juice.

And chicken bones fresh for the plucking.

She tapped her broom and counted to ten.

Swiss cheese, onion rings, peanut butter. Abby heard a click and a squawk and a scratch of claws. The bird rattled in the can, scraping bottom. Abby dropped her broom and ran for the lid. It slammed shut, nice and snug, with her perched on top. For certainty. She drummed the sides of the can and said, 'I've got you now, magpie.'

The chocolate Lab lifted his head.

Abby carried the garbage can into the yard, placing it right next to that stiff broom. She turned that broom upside down and opened the lid just enough to slide the handle in.

Dirty garbage can.

The magpie was angry, so Abby pushed down hard. She pushed, stabbed and poked, and the magpie clacked, squawked and gagged.

A real gerbil in a coffee tin.

The broom swayed under her weight. The thrust of her shoulders snapped the handle to a point. She stabbed the magpie. The chocolate Lab jumped, barked and gnashed his teeth. He yelped and teetered the fence.

Away with the dirty broom, and Abby sat on top of the garbage can again, holding its lid tight, until the cacophony tuned a tender whistle. The Lab rested his chin on the dry grass while Abby grabbed the magpie by the neck.

Twitchy warm fingers.

Abby slapped the carcass upon the counter, a slight pulse to the beak. Then a paring knife from the butcher's block cut through a breast of feathers. The bone cracked and spilled blood, so she cut over a bowl to catch it. Prying chest to guts, she said, 'Where did you put my ring? No old bird steals my ring!'

Jammed wrist deep, she pinched at a new green potato of a stomach. She sliced the new green potato down the middle. It let out a hiss. Squinting her eyes and attempting not to breathe, Abby saw a paper clip, a rusty nail, some jellybeans and a chicken wing. But no ring.

Young Young Miss Lamp picked up a shiny black-blue and greenish feather, white near the quill. She twirled it in her fingers. 'What are you making, Mom?'

Abby pressed the bird down into the bowl.

§

The Hollywood Bowl.

Game six is a close one. Banana Tray Hair's coaching ability is innate – she's a born leader. 'Aim for the third arrow, Soupy! Third arrow! Do it, Soupy. Do it!' His second strike in a row prompts the blue screen of their scoreboard to flash:

SOUPY

SOUPY

SOUPY

STEE-RIKE!!!

Knocking all pins clear, he spins round on his bowling shoes and wipes the strike from his hands. Banana Tray Hair marvels at his form. 'A natural underhand you are, Soupy. Impressive.' Room Service Boy responds well to the call of 'Soupy.' The fact that she notices his underhand prowess allows him to remove his purple suit coat, roll up his cuffs evenly and straighten his purple dickie bow tie.

The other kids make fun of Room Service Boy and his girlish underhand toss, but Banana Tray Hair sees potential. Pure bowling-league potential. 'Come on over and have another drink,' she says. The sound of rattling pins keeps his head warm.

'And this one? Is it a short, short glass of chocolate milk?' He takes a sniff. 'Smells like coffee. If it's coffee, ma'am, I don't drink coffee. Much too dangerous. I can't be shaky on the job.'

'It's a B-52.'

Room Service Boy's black-and-white war documentaries about dive-bombers soar to Banana Tray Hair's bra in Technicolor. He observes the strap. Pink dive-bombers.

'Have I tried this kind yet?'

'Nope.' Banana Tray Hair knows her drinks. Raising her shooter glass, she clinks it with his and says, 'Bombs away.'

Room Service Boy thinks she's pretty hot. 'Exactly what I would have said.' Room Service Boy impresses easily.

Banana Tray Hair dabs her lips on the back of her hand. 'You're supposed to drink too!'

'Oh. Sorry, Lucy, ma'am.'

'My turn.' Sauntering up to the lane hand dryer, Banana Tray Hair rubs her hands dry. A real cracked thumb. She scoops up a swirly ball, examines it for nicks and gives her shoulders a purposeful shrug. 'Keep it loose, baby. Keep it loose.' The alley simmers to a din. She parks the toes of her special bowling shoes at the red line of Lane 4. Her release hand lines up perfectly with the third arrow from the left. She lets out a sigh and peers down the lane. A collective whisper grows louder.

'Lu-cy, Lu-cy, Lu-cy.'

'Oh, that tastes good.' Room Service Boy wipes B-52 off his chin, spins his head around the room and grips tight to his orange plastic chair. He loves to watch her step.

'Lu-cy, Lu-cy, Lu-cy.' The patrons of the Lanes know a good strike when they see one.

Banana Tray Hair pushes her hair out of her face and takes five generous steps back, keeping her eye on the mark. She points her free hand to the side with a slight bend of the knees. She leans into her shot with a push of thigh and cocks her release hand square to her shoulder, cradling the ball. She tunes out the chant, the chatter, the nerves, and begins her departure. 'Mama needs a new pair of shoes.'

With ballerina toes and a slingshot arm, she sets the ball on its mission.

A rolling kaleidoscope.

The ball twists out a wet drum roll, hydroplaning veneer, carving a line like the letter I in a strong west wind – all the way home. The west coast, she calls it. Splash. The pins heave to the floor in a mighty clatter. A two-four split. Very tricky.

§

Say It with Flowers.

Young Miss Lamp stormed down the sidewalk, the dusty breeze stinging her eyes. Pica picked at shards of green glass nestled against the curb as the sky threatened to spill upon Young Miss Lamp's yellow dress.

Rush hour.

Warm water and Ajax soaked through the belly of her dress. 'That's going to stain too,' she said, scowling at her wet belly, hiding the grey circle with her hand. 'Great.'

Slinging her well-contained red purse behind her shoulder, she passed the brick wall where Paper Boy got his thirty-fifth dollar. She passed the pawn shop where Paper Boy got his seventieth dollar. She passed Paper Boy, who held flowers for her. His head in orchids. Hers in her dress.

Smelling a peach on the breeze, Paper Boy caught a flash of yellow and threw his body into a quick reverse. Walking backward down the sidewalk brought his toes to heel. His fistful of flowers brushed lightly against her chin. His T-shirt was nearly dry as he breathed out and in.

Her head turned to petals.

'Here,' he huffed. 'For you they are.'

His fist pulled the orchids away. Her chin pushed them closer.

'Waiting I was ... ask if you to – '

Her chin pushed them closer. Toe to heel.

Paper Boy righted himself. Heel to toe.

'These are for you.'

Stamens tickled her nose. 'They're gorgeous. Very robust.'

The rain crinkled in wax paper.

'Where did you go?'

'To the dentist.'

'I've got some more money here for you, and some food. Have you had lunch yet?' She searched in her well-contained red purse.

Paper Boy squeaked like a reed. 'I am a bit peckish.'

Pawn Shop Man was eating his lunch.

As Young Miss Lamp held out a Tootsie Roll, Paper Boy broke a sweat. 'I, I can't eat a Tootsie Roll, I'm afraid.'

'Oh. Silly me. You were just at the dentist's. Oops.' Butterflies flew into her stomach as passersby aplenty opened up their steel-tipped umbrellas to catch the leaky sky, to stop it before it hit their shoes. Young Miss Lamp thought the band-aids on Paper Boy's cheek added character. Almost a wink's worth.

'Where's your jacket?'

'I sold it.'

'To who?'

Paper Boy pointed up the street to the pawn shop. The breeze snuck right up his arm. Chicken skin.

Young Miss Lamp was a real fox. 'My mom is such a bitch. She yelled at me for ten minutes because of the stupid stain on my dress.' The rain speckled her shoulders.

Paper Boy connected the dots.

Cinnamon on skin.

'You can hardly notice it.'

Paper Boy's hair needed a good scrubbing, but Young Miss Lamp knew how to receive a compliment. 'That's what I said.'

'What did she say?'

'She said the dress was ruined. She said I wreck all my best clothes. It's not ruined, is it?' The dots upon her yellow dress multiplied.

'No. It all looks nice.' Paper Boy was really connecting.

'That's what I said. She's such a bitch.' Young Miss Lamp rolled out her shoulders as rivulets of rain ate at her red-suede shoes.

Cinnamon toast.

'Well. I've got money now, so let's go buy your jacket back.' She grabbed Paper Boy by the wrist as they scuffed back up the sidewalk. Those bloody doodles on his wrists weren't quite dry yet.

'Would you like your flowers now?' he asked.

§

Lucy's Diamond Necklace Cabaret.

                          'You sure cleaned up a nasty two-four split, m'Lucy.'

'I was in the trenches, Soupy.'

'Did you plan it out?'

'No time to plan. Those pins are tricky. I was working my west coast.'

Retiring to the Lanes' lounge after a hard day's bowl soothes Banana Tray Hair's constitution. Their blue drinks have a yellow umbrella and a tiny red straw in each. Room Service Boy's difficulty with straws tells her he's a hands-on kind of man. His panache in placing the umbrella behind his ear suggests a desire for excitement.

His drink smells like coconuts.

Hers like vacation.

She admires his honesty and his underhand toss. Carrying tray after tray in the hotel. Definitely strong wrists. And well-dressed.

Five-pin in style, indeed.

Banana Tray Hair deserves a man who can handle himself in a bowling alley.

'Have you ever considered joining a team?' Her straw moves to her tongue.

'Sure is a lot of pressure.' His umbrella slips behind his ear.

'You could join my team.' Her hand squeezing his knee allows for some consideration in joining her team. 'You're a natural. You hit five strikes tonight. Five. Three is normally acceptable for a first date. But five is very efficient.' She nods in agreement with herself, in awe of Room Service Boy's upper lip.

A blue coconut-milk moustache.

'Have you ever considered taking six steps back instead of five? It might be more efficient, ma'am.'

'Old!'

Room Service Boy prides himself on his efficiency. He can finish an entire syrupy drink in one sip. 'So have you?

'I have.'

'Ah.'

'Tastes like another? Well?' Banana Tray Hair likes her drinks. 'You're about to lose your umbrella. Let me – '

Banana Tray Hair's pink bra strap hides freckles, Room Service Boy notices. 'Thanks, Lucy, my oh my.' He checks above his ear and spills a tablespoon smile. Pure vanilla. As she drifts to the bar to get two more drinks, he smiles enough to fill a soup spoon twice over. She drifts back rather speedily. These drinks are not blue. There are no umbrellas or straws. This time the drinks are on fire.

'Quick. Quick.' Banana Tray Hair sets down the small tray of flaming drinks.

Room Service Boy drops his jaw. 'Your hair!'

'My hair?' It's always salon fresh when she checks it in the mirror.

'Your hair! Your hair! Safety!' Taking his very own hand, Room Service Boy pats her smouldering curls with vigour.

'Oh shit! Quick! The drinks! Blow the flame out first.'

He blows out both of the flames, for safety.

'To Vegas!' Banana Tray Hair raises her glass. Clink, clink.

In less than two seconds Room Service Boy replies, 'Wow. That tastes good. What's it called?'

'A flaming sambuca.' She owns a guide to mixology.

'Not a Vegas?' He doesn't own an atlas.

'No, silly. Vegas is where I'm going for a holiday.'

'Your hair was on fire.'

'Thanks, Soupy.' Leaning to, she gives him a kiss on his licorice lips until his umbrella falls out. 'It happened last week too. Maybe I should get a haircut. Too dangerous.'

Moving fro, he says, 'Your hair is nice.'

She picks out the burnt bits while he hovers above his drink.

'I'm going to Vegas. To a show. It has my name in it. And diamonds.' Her flourish of fingers fans the smell of lemons, not burnt wool. 'It stars Lucy – c'est moi – and her Diamond Necklace Cabaret. It's supposed to be fantastic and it runs for two weeks straight! I have all the information at home. Their big number is called "Why I Hate the Romans," with fifty soldier boys onstage and they're all wearing diamonds! Maybe you could come with me.'

Room Service Boy has never been to Vegas, and he's pretty sure he doesn't hate the Romans. 'How many Air Miles does it take?' he asks.

§

Facts of the Day.

Mrs. Lane delights in the facts of the day. 'Oh my,' she says, sipping her orange pekoe. Tepid. The headline shouts at her:

HOTSHOT LAWYER FREES MAD DENTIST

'Did you see this, honey?'

Mr. Lane reads his facts of the day in the afternoon.

'No, dear.' He is late for work. Reading in the morning increases his chances of being late for work.

'It's about that dentist who steals people's teeth. He's free, apparently.'

'How's my tie?' Mr. Lane has a massive head. It is vital his tie be centred, so as not to make one side of the head appear larger than the other. Mrs. Lane continues to read.

There were few celebrating the verdict passed down by the Peachland District Court yesterday afternoon – except savvy defence lawyer Miss Lamp and her notorious client, Dr. Delano.

'Honey, I'm squinting again,' she says. 'Do you remember where I put my glasses?'

'How's my tie?'

Mrs. Lane examines his head-to-tie ratio, up and down, left to right. 'It's crooked. Have you seen my glasses?'

Undoing his tie, Mr. Lane remembers where she put her glasses. 'I don't think he ever went to jail. He did fool around with our neighbour's wife, though.'

'My glasses. Did you see them this morning?'

'They're beside your teacup.'

'Oh. Thanks.' Sliding specs up the bridge of her nose, she reads the kitchen clock. 'Aren't you late for work?'

Mr. Lane flips his tie around, over and through its loop. 'Yes.'

'Better hurry up then.' Returning her gaze to the paper, she sighs in relief. 'Now I can see. Much better. Now where was I?'

Judge Sam Daniel condemned the crown prosecutor's case alleging fraud, malpractice and theft over $2000 against 'mad dentist' Dr. Amasa Delano as 'weak,' 'ill-founded' and 'simply preposterous.'

Local victims' advocacy representative Ms. Harper was outraged by the decision. 'Where are the people's teeth?' she asked.

Dr. Delano, a local dentist, was widely rumoured to have hoarded his clients' gold teeth – without consent – for several decades. Police investigations of his premises proved unfruitful.

'The evidence simply wasn't there,' said Chief Detective Constable Johnson.

'They say there's no evidence.' Mrs. Lane slurps at her tea. 'But he must have hidden them somewhere.'

The detective was part of a team tracking the movements of Dr. Delano. 'We kept pretty close tabs on him,' he said. 'Other than a few minor traffic violations and operating a bicycle while intoxicated, he kept his nose clean.' Constable Johnson later added, 'He really enjoys his drink. I'm not sure I'd have him as my dentist.'

'I heard he keeps them in a shoebox.' Mr. Lane fixes his knot, pressing his tie flat. 'How's that?'

Mrs. Lane re-examines his head-to-tie ratio. 'He's drunk all the time, apparently. A little to the left – can you imagine? A drunk dentist!'

Mrs. Jones, a former long-time client of the now-exonerated dentist, gave evidence on behalf of several 'victims' who were either too elderly or incapacitated to attend the proceedings, including former town councillor Dick Harper, who is currently recovering in hospital from a rare case of flesh-eating disease.

'He doesn't have flesh-eating disease. Dick Harper lost his leg in a bear trap.'

'Same thing, isn't it?'

'I suppose so. A smidge more to the left.'

'How's the tie now?'

'Perfect.' Mrs. Lane looks up at her man in the morning and returns to the facts of the day.

A visibly shaken Mrs. Jones commented, 'We demand our fair shake. We want our precious teeth back. Some of us had diamonds in our mouths.'

Observers said Mrs. Jones had to be restrained several times during the deliberations. She remains confident about appealing Judge Daniel's decision: 'That [judge's] decision was wrong. Delano kept our teeth to profit for himself, with no regard for our property or dental health whatsoever – that maggot will be back in court again very, very soon.'

In stark contrast to ...

'Give us a kiss before you go, honey.'

The girth of Mr. Lane's head forces him to put his hands on the table when Mrs. Lane puckers up her orange-pekoe lips. He really leans on the table. 'You've spilled your tea, honey.'

§

How Much Are Those Shoes in the Alley?

Young Young Miss Lamp slid down the wooden steps, bump, bump, bump to the front hall. She pulled herself up using the banister, stretching for the wooden screen door.

Almost.

She fell to her knees with Denis Brown Splints in tow.

A green inchworm.

She squirmed to the porch swing, determined to walk in her shoes. 'One lap around the fence,' she declared, and down the porch step she went. Bump.

The grass was prickly underhand.

The inchworm wiggled to white washboards. Wiggled enough to get her fingers between the slats. She winched herself along in a sliver or two.

The chocolate Lab lifted his head and blew out through his nose.

Young Young Miss Lamp hopped and heaved past the willow tree, twisted and strained at the slats of the fence. As easy as monkey bars.

'These shoes don't make me walk better.'

The shiny brass bar connecting two tiny patent-leather shoes ground into the earth, ploughing a trail of dust.

'I'll make them walk better,' she said, as her arms started to burn.

With a patch over one eye, Grandma polished the living-room window with a crumpled-up newspaper and a sprinkle of vinegar. Her eye stayed close to the glass as she picked out smudges to attack. 'Goddamn Abby, can't keep her windows clean.' Grandma had never cleaned the outside of a window in her life. She chugged from her pint glass of vinegar, coughing spit all over her fine work.

'Such a mess,' she said. Her voice sounded something awful. A kidney on the grindstone.

The sunlight bore out her wrinkles.

She knocked back another sip, pouring the rest on the newspaper.

Throat dry as rock salt.

Scouring the window, she caught a sparkle in the dust, a trail of shiny brass moving next to the fence. She dropped her newspaper and pressed her eye firm to the pane to be sure, blinking a greasy smudge. 'Is that a Lamp?'

When Grandma dropped her half-pint of vinegar, the glass bit her toes. She never wore shoes in the house.

Young Young Miss Lamp marked the corner of the fence with a grin. Then she tried moving backward for the stretch to the alley gate, but it didn't work. Twisting her body back around, she sprung to the fence like a gymnast. 'Nadia Comaneci,' she said as she gathered a collection of slivers, scraping her bare elbows along the way.

Her feet fell out from under her.

Grandma had the shiny brass bar in her grip. Young Young Miss Lamp's soft, tiny fingers slid down the rough wood. Her chin met a heap of dry grass. 'No, Grandma! No!' Young Young Miss Lamp was nearly finished her lap.

Grandma pulled as hard as a fence board. 'Give me those ugly things. You little monster!' She was determined to get those Denis Brown Splints.

'No, Grandma! They help me walk!'

Grandma started to huff. 'Let go of the goddamn fence or I'll rip your arms off!'

'No! Stop!' The gymnast held tight, her arms as strong as pipes.

'I'll teach you to walk!' Grandma huffed and puffed. 'No granddaughter of mine is going to be in a circus! Let go!' The fence nails squeaked away their rust.

The chocolate Lab barked and barked, digging at the dirt beneath his tiny window. Pica picked at the grass next to Grandma's purple varicose feet. Her pinky toe glistened in the sunshine.

Abby was in the kitchen, cooking chicken and boiling broccoli, counting well over a minute to herself.

Soggy broccoli for Grandma, and the fence board was really starting to give.

Young Young Miss Lamp's arms stretched red, her ankles turning blue.

'Those ugly shoes can't teach you how to walk.' Grandma put her back into her work.

Abby cleared steam away from the kitchen window with her tea towel. Then she dropped the pot of broccoli in the sink and ran out the door in a smack.

'Mom. Help!'

Abby stopped in the middle of the yard. 'Stop it! You're hurting her! Let go of her shoes this instant!'

Grandma focused her eye. 'Go away, Abby. I'm teaching your daughter to – ' Grandma leaned straight back. ' – to walk.'

Young Young Miss Lamp let go of the fence because the fence let go of its nails, and Grandma dropped to the grass.

'Mom!' Young Young Miss Lamp's little face was dirty.

Abby snapped her tea towel at Grandma.

'You have to undo the laces first. The laces!'

Grandma continued to tug at the bar. 'Get those shoes off!'

'I'll do it. Move!' Abby grabbed Grandma's broken ring finger, prying it from the shiny bar.

'Ow. Don't you touch me, Abby Lamp.'

Pica bobbed up clouds of dust on his way to Grandma's pinky toe. He snapped at its glossy nail with his beak. 'Ahhh!' Grandma gargled in her salty spit, her tear ducts vinegar-dry. She hid under the willow tree.

The laces of the Denis Brown Splints loosened with Abby's picking, relieving the pressure from her daughter's hot, sore feet.

'Mom.'

'Yes, dear.'

'Grandma did this before. In my room.'

Abby pulled off the sweltering shoes, fixed together at fifty and one hundred and thirty degrees respectively. The brass bar kept them true.

'Why were you wearing these outside? They're for sleeping!' Denis Brown Splints are expensive.

'I nearly finished my lap.'

Above the garbage can, Pica said hello to Young Young Miss Lamp. From the fence he clicked and squawked, loud as a magpie. He shuffled his talons in a sidestep, swaying his body the direction of his sharp, dark eyes.

The chocolate Lab growled, and Grandma shook under the tree.

A wisp in the willows.

Abby's red locks were frazzled. Real licorice whips.

Pica screeched again.

'Shut up. Oh, shut up!' Abby picked up the special shoes. 'Go away, magpie! I don't have anything for you!'

Pica danced on top of the fence, leering at her red licorice. He teased her with his saunter and strut, flashing tail feathers of black-blue and shiny green. White near the quill.

With both hands, Abby swung the Denis Brown Splints over her head, launching them clear of the yard and clear of the fence.

Pica didn't flinch.

§

When a Stranger Calls.

A knock at the door brings Miss Lamp to her feet, balance askew. Her ear has been ringing all morning. She can't even look at a Q-tip.

'Who is it?'

Hotel people always announce themselves.

'Room service.'

She hasn't ordered breakfast yet.

'Hold on a minute.' She picks up the phone very carefully, holding it a safe distance from her good ear.

'Hello?'

'A visitor to see you, ma'am.'

'Pardon me?' His voice sounds fresh, she thinks.

'A visitor to see you, ma'am.'

'You mean it isn't you?'

'No, ma'am. A visitor. He rode his ten-speed right into the lobby.'

'Oh.' Returning the receiver to its cradle, Miss Lamp takes a heavy terry housecoat from its hanger, wrapping herself tight. Her thin green-rimmed glasses sit on the table. The door clicks open in a whoosh.

Mothballs and tea.

And port.

Miss Lamp plays safe.

Delano bounces in his britches. A sailor in the crow's nest.

'The bellboy in the purple suit sure has a nice smile. Nice young fella. Looks a lot like me, don't you think?'

'No.' Miss Lamp thinks of Room Service Boy's upper lip.

Peach fuzz.

'Did you read the facts of the day? Hot off the presses. Got mine before the sun rose this morning. Four-fifteen to be exact.

Got a hundred of 'em. One hundred. Make way. Make way.' Delano makes way, all right, all the way to the foot of Miss Lamp's bed. His swinging wingtips barely touch the berber. 'Got one for you right here, lady. Front-page news I am. Have yourself a look and see. They call me mad but now I'm free!'

Miss Lamp doesn't remember Delano being capable of rhyme.

While Miss Lamp grabs for her glasses, Delano removes a newspaper from his inside pocket, two from his outside pockets, then slides his pant leg up and removes one from his argyle sock. He hands that one to her.

'Thanks.' She places it on the table. The yellow plastic daisy in the plastic daisy holder is in her travel bag.

'Hot off the presses.' The tooth he and Mr. Harper shared is still missing as he bounces up and down on the foot of her bed. His tongue lolls out in a wag.

'Read it. Read it! Mrs. Jones called me a maggot. I'm not a maggot.' Delano can hardly contain himself. 'I'm a dentist, and Mrs. Jones wears dentures now.' As Miss Lamp scrutinizes the article, Delano produces a rose-velvet ring box from his breast pocket. He offers the ring box to her.

'For me?' Miss Lamp's still wet behind the ears.

'Open it. Open it!' Delano's port is dry.

'Wow.' Miss Lamp holds a ruby set in a gold incisor atop a shimmering band of white gold. 'Really, you shouldn't have. The box is lovely.' Miss Lamp doesn't wear rings.

'It's my own tooth – I made the ring myself.' Delano hoists his line. 'For all your super work, and your winning smile, and if you ever need a – '

'I have a dentist.' Miss Lamp's dentist is a stranger.

'Oh.' Delano battens up his sadness, allowing the first words that catch wind to sail out of his mouth. 'That shaky lady sure cried a lot. Abby. I remember her first checkup. Bad teeth. Smelly shoes.

The needle wasn't rusty. Right?' Delano rubs his teeth with the back of his tie. Oakum between the deck planks.

Placing the ring box into Delano's hand, Miss Lamp finds the patience to let herself breathe. So Miss Lamp tells him, 'That lady is my mother.'

'Hmm.' Delano closes his soft hand to sad velvet.

No sale.

Mindful of teeth piling up in his backyard, he asks, 'Do you know of any good accountants?'

§

Miss Lamp Reads Herself.

Miss Lamp unfolds the facts of the day upon her twin bed, laughing about Delano's ring. 'Can you imagine? Where could I wear that?'

With the money she saved the insurance company, she fantasizes about a holiday. In a shiver, she pulls up the covers and floats on her back.

She could get another music box for her mother.

Holding the paper above her head, Miss Lamp begins to read:

HOTSHOT LAWYER FREES MAD DENTIST

Touching her finger to her thigh, she lets out a sizzle. Miss Lamp reads the parts about herself first.

> In stark contrast to Mrs. Jones's outrage, star defence lawyer Miss Lamp was pleased with the decision. Pausing outside the courthouse for photographs and questions from reporters, she shrugged and said, 'I'm not going to lie to you: removing a patient's tooth and replacing it with a much safer plastic composite is not a crime. The man was simply doing his job. And he's been doing that job well for over forty years.'

'I think I'd insist on commas before and after "well,"' she says.

> Miss Lamp was quickly shuttled back to her hotel, where she had prepared her client's case for some time. Asked to comment on the lawyer's behaviour, the hotel staff representative remarked, 'We haven't seen her in days.'
>
> A local paper delivery boy concurred that Miss Lamp was behaving rather oddly. 'Witnesses often had to repeat their statements,' he said. 'She looked dizzy.'

A local doctor indicated that he might have treated the lawyer for an unspecified ear injury.

Pushing at her ear to muffle the ring, she scowls. 'I will be in touch with you, doctor.' She is not going to lie to him – he's not very bright.

Judge Daniel remarked, 'The case for the defence was airtight. The accusations by the crown were weak, ill-founded and utterly preposterous. That man has been a shining example of adequate dentistry in this community for decades.'

Dr. Delano was rather glib when asked how he would celebrate his victory, stating, 'With a drink, of course.'

Confronted with allegations of tooth theft on such a massive scale, he remarked, 'If it has to come out, it has to come out.'

Miss Lamp hopes Delano will keep teeth in people's mouths. She's not planning to come back to the Peachland Hotel anytime soon, although she finds the peaches quite delicious.

After thanking his lawyer, he was quick to unlock his ten-speed bicycle, speeding away from Mrs. Jones and her supporters.

In a related matter, Dr. Delano was also cleared of allegations of professional negligence surrounding a personal-injury claim stemming from an incident years earlier.

'Too much time has passed since the incident in question,' Judge Daniel ruled. 'The medical evidence presented by noted physiologist Dr. Steeves was insubstantial.'

The unnamed plaintiff suffers from nerve damage, allegedly caused by a dirty needle used by Dr. Delano. The plaintiff's insurance company – also represented by Miss Lamp – has refused to pay damages of any sort, including medication.

Miss Lamp folds up the paper and thinks about ordering another grilled cheese and Campbell's Tomato Soup from Room Service Boy. She knows it comes with a pickle. It's too early for lunch in her flannel Mountie pyjamas, but she reminds herself to order some juice to wash it down. Peach juice.

Stretching her toes to the edge of her bed, she feels as though she hasn't left Room 32 for days.

§

Acknowledgements.

    Miss Lamp would not exist without the sustenance of the Calgary writing community and those who support it. We are growing.

Thanks to all at Coach House Books for making my book a book: my editor, Alana Wilcox, for turning on to *Miss Lamp* and polishing *Miss Lamp* to a shine, Christina Palassio for finding it places to do so, and Stan Bevington for keeping the lights on.

I owe a debt of gratitude to the assiduous Aritha van Herk – a remarkable teacher of keeping the lines in line and letting them loose when need be. Thank you for believing.

Thanks to my mom and dad, Patricia and Gary Ewart, for their support, understanding and confidence in me – and to my brother, Geoff, for showing me the importance of reading innovative literature.

Miss Sandy Ann Lam, your patience, creativity and unwavering support inspires me to no end. Lucky indeed.

I want to be as cool as Larissa Lai when I grow up. Thanks for helping me get mine.

Nicole Markotić was the first to teach me that fiction and poetry are, at times, inseparable. Thank you for your support too.

Thanks also to Meagan Lang for that spark, and to Jeremy Leipert and André Rodrigues for knocking on my door that fine spring day.

More thanks to Derek Beaulieu, Nancy Tousley, Natalee Caple, Stephen Cain at Insomniac Press, Suzette Mayr, Julia Williams, *filling Station*, Jocelyn Grossé and *bemused*, NO Press, Christian Bök, Natalie Walschots and Jordan Nail at *dANDelion*, Eric Moschopedis and Bubonic Tourist, Jordan Scott, Ryan Fitzpatrick, Paul Kennett, Jill Hartman, Jason Christie, Crystal Mimura, Jani Krulc, Frances Kruk, Travis Murphy, James

Dangerous, Cara Hedley, Jessica Grant, Weyman Chan, Mark Hopkins, Jonathan Ball, Ed Schmutz, Andrea Ryer, William Neil Scott, Lee Depner, Aaron Giovannone, Harry Vandervlist, Fred Wah, Victor Ramraj, Florentine Strzelczyk, Clem Martini, Tom Wayman, Jane Chamberlain-Grove, Phil Rivard, Kathryn Sloan, Heather Ellwood-Wright, Xay Saysana, Deb Steplock, the Kathleen and Russell Lane Canadian Writing Scholarship, Literary Kaleidoscope, Pages Books on Kensington, McNally Robinson Booksellers, Alberta Magazine Publishers Association, the support of the English Department at the University of Calgary and my friends there, my colleagues at the Department of Communication and Culture and the Effective Writing Centre, the Renert Centre, Equilibrium International Education Institute, Kensington Pub, The Stoop, my old laptop and the many wonderful students I teach and learn from.

About the Author.

Chris Ewart was born in Encino, California, grew up in Mississauga, Ontario, went to music school in London, Ontario, travelled to over twenty-five countries and now lives in Calgary. He recently completed an MA in English at the University of Calgary, where he teaches effective writing. He is also a frequent contributor to the *Calgary Herald*'s Books and the Arts section. His creative works appear in numerous publications including *orange, bemused, filling Station,* No Press, Emeritus Press, *It's Still Winter – A Journal of Contemporary Canadian Poetics* and *NōD*. His short story 'Her Belly Matches the Table' was nominated for the 2002 Journey Prize in Literature, and he received the Kathleen and Russell Lane Canadian Writing Scholarship in 2004. His play *Billy's Drums* is in development with Calgary's FireBelly Theatre for 2007 and he is currently working on a collection of poems and a second novel.

Typeset in Legacy and Legacy Sans
Printed and bound at the Coach House on bpNichol Lane, 2006

Edited and designed by Alana Wilcox
Author photo by Sandy Lam

Coach House Books
401 Huron Street on bpNichol Lane
Toronto, Ontario, Canada
M5S 2G5

800 367 6360
416 979 2217

mail@chbooks.com
www.chbooks.com